*WILL*

*YE LET*

*THE MUMMERS*

*IN?*

# WILL YE LET THE MUMMERS IN?

STORIES BY

## ALDEN NOWLAN

with a preface by ROBERT WEAVER

IRWIN PUBLISHING
Toronto   Canada

Copyright © *Irwin Publishing Inc., 1984*
Introduction Copyright © 1984 by Robert Weaver

**Canadian Cataloguing in Publication Data**

Nowlan, Alden, 1933-1983.
  Will ye let the mummers in?

ISBN 0-7720-1407-8

1. Title

PS8527.084W54 1984     C813'.54     C84-098246-1
PR9199.3.N68W54 1984

Designed by Robert Burgess Garbutt
Typeset by Century Typesetting Inc
Printed in Canada by T. H. Best

1 2 3 4 5 6 7 8 THB 91 90 89 88 87 86 85 84

*Published by Irwin Publishing Inc.*

*For Johnnie and Claudine with love*
*and to David Adams Richards*
*and Robert Weaver*

# CONTENTS

*PREFACE* by Robert Weaver      ix

The Fall of a City      *1*
Nightmare      *8*
Liar, Liar      *13*
Skipper      *17*
Girls and Women, Boys and Men      *23*
The Persistence of Theodore Roosevelt      *28*
One Cold Bright Afternoon      *34*
The Thin Red Line      *38*
Cynthia Loves You      *43*
The Insurance Man      *49*

Hello Out There     *54*
Will Ye Let the Mummers In?     *60*
A Jukebox in the Kitchen     *76*
Prisoner of War     *81*
The Year of the Revolution     *84*
Infidelity     *98*
True Confession     *110*
The Question     *114*
Mother and Son     *121*
Walking on the Ceiling     *128*
Morning Flight to Red Deer     *141*
About Memorials     *150*

# ACKNOWLEDGEMENTS

*MANY* of the stories in this collection were previously published, usually in a somewhat different form, between 1960 and 1982 in the following magazines: *The Atlantic Advocate, Atlantic Insight, The Canadian Fiction Magazine, Canadian Forum, The Dalhousie Review, Dandelion, Fiddlehead, Hanging Loose, The Journal of Canadian Fiction, Pottersfield Portfolio, Prism International, Pluck, Queen's Quarterly,* and *Waves.* Three have been broadcast on CBC radio. The author also wishes to acknowledge a short-term grant from the Canada Council during the preparation of the final manuscript, and the creative criticism of his friend Nancy Bauer.

# PREFACE

ALDEN NOWLAN had gathered together
this collection of short stories before his death, in June
1983 at the age of 50, in Fredericton, New Brunswick. He
was best known as a poet, who had won a Governor
General's Award for poetry for *Bread, Wine and Salt* in
1967, and who was admired by fellow poets in Canada
and the United States and by those of us who became
simply his faithful readers. But he wrote fiction and plays
as well as the poetry. *Will Ye Let the Mummers In?* is
Nowlan's second collection of stories. An earlier book of
short fiction, *Miracle at Indian River,* was published in
1968 and in a paperback edition in 1982. He also wrote a
"fictional memoir" *Various Persons Named Kevin*

*O'Brien* (1973), a memorable portrait of Maritimes village life.

For a time in the 1970s Nowlan embarked on a new writing career when he collaborated with the director Walter Learning on three theatre plays: *Frankenstein, The Dollar Woman,* and *The Incredible Murder of Cardinal Tosca. The Dollar Woman* was taken from a strange, disreputable incident in the social history of New Brunswick. But the other plays were entertainments that the two authors must have approached with a good deal of elaborate fun in mind. Perhaps these plays belonged partly to that side of Alden Nowlan's nature that caused him to become for a time the manager of a country music band. He said later of this experience that "the main problem with the band was keeping them sober enough to play: 'George Shaw and the Green Valley Ranch Boys' — they were good, too." He was a writer, and a man, of many, sometimes contradictory parts.

His early life might easily have made him the most sombre of writers. He was born, not in New Brunswick but in Nova Scotia, in one of the worst years of the Depression. In 1969 the Fredericton literary magazine *The Fiddlehead* published an issue entirely devoted to Alden Nowlan and his work. In an interview for that issue Nowlan said of his early life: "In many ways it was 19th Century, a pioneer environment: no electric light or telephones, nothing like that . . . That country around Stanley wasn't like the Annapolis Valley; the soil was too poor for farming. The people there were mostly pulp-cutters. A great feeling of insecurity all the time. My father was born in 1904, and he's always wanted to work, but he's never had a permanent job . . ." A terrible Maritimes story, made all the more terrible by the fact that the "great feeling of insecurity" is there once again today in so many parts of Nova Scotia and New Brunswick.

Nowlan left school in grade 5 and worked cutting pulp,

and as a night watchman in a sawmill, and for the Nova Scotia Department of Highways (one of his books of poetry, *The Mysterious Naked Man,* includes "Two Poems for the Nova Scotia Department of Highways"). Later Nowlan emigrated to New Brunswick, where he worked on newspapers, first on the *Hartland Observer* in a town upriver from Fredericton (it was also in Hartland that he became manager of the country music band), and then on the *Telegraph-Journal* in Saint John. In 1968 he became writer-in-residence at the University of New Brunswick in Fredericton, and he lived in a house on the edge of the campus for the remainder of his life, a long association that does credit to the university.

Given Alden Nowlan's childhood in a thin-soil area of Nova Scotia, and his adult life spent in the small towns and not-very-large cities of New Brunswick — and the depth of his response to this experience — it's inevitable that he has been seen to be, and indeed was, a regional writer. But he is a regional writer as, say, Jack Hodgins is on the West Coast or Alice Munro in Ontario: writers who are anchored in a particular place in Canada, but who also belong to the international literary community. As a poet, Alden Nowlan had strong emotional ties with William Carlos Williams and other American poets, and I do not think that he would be displeased when I say that his stories belong to a tradition that goes back at least as far as Sherwood Anderson's great "book of the grotesque", *Winesburg, Ohio.* Nowlan's poems and stories about life in the Maritimes were written from the vantage point of a sophisticated, well read, quirky, independent, and stubborn mind.

He once wrote that the long narrative poem was not his most natural mode. A similar comment might be made about his fiction. One or two of the stories in this collection — "Will Ye Let the Mummers In?", and the satire on universities and intellectual fashion, "The Year of the Revolution" — are what might be described as traditional short stories. But for the most part we have here a group of sketches; glimpses of life in the Maritimes that complement many of Nowlan's best known poems. Loneliness, isolation and retreat into a fantasy world, are the subject matter of "The Fall of a City" and "Hello, Out There". Two stories that might have been conceived as a pair, "Skipper" and "True Confession", are almost sociological documents, showing us what happens to people whose work brings them no joy and no prospect of escape. But Alden Nowlan wasn't a sociologist, he had a poet's imagination, and the society he knew so well was full of strange and unexpected twists. Consider "The Insurance man", perhaps my favourite of all the sketches in this book. The Maritimes seem to have their quota of native sons who have come back to retire after successful professional careers abroad, but surely few of them have a history as odd as that of Pegiel Tucker.

In the mid-1960s Alden Nowlan very nearly died of cancer. He survived and lived on for almost two decades, but the shadow of that illness falls across a number of his poems and stories like "Walking on the Ceiling". He still died too young: we can't help regretting the poems that were not written, the stories not even begun. But he left an enduring writer's legacy behind him: the poems and stories that will be read again and again. *Will Ye Let the Mummers In?* is a significant part of that legacy.

Robert Weaver
Toronto
March 1984

# THE FALL
# OF A CITY

*OUTSIDE, RAIN FELL* with such violence that great, pulsating sheets of water seemed to hang suspended between earth and sky. Squatting in the attic, Teddy watched raindrops roll like beads of quicksilver down the glass of the high, diamond-shaped window, and listened to the muted banjo twanging on the roof.

Blinking, he shifted his position and transferred his attention to the things that lay around him on the floor. In the centre of the room stood a fort and a palace, painstakingly constructed from corrugated cardboard cartons. These were surrounded by humbler dwellings made from matchboxes and the covers of exercise books. The streets and alleys were full of nobles, peasants and

1

soldiers, their two-dimensional bodies scissored from paper, their faces and clothing drawn in crayon and lead pencil. From the turreted roof of the palace hung a blue, white and gold tricolour, the flag of the Kingdom of Upalia. . .

Sombre grey eyes glinted in Teddy's pale triangular face. He shoved his hands deeper in the pockets of his worn khaki shorts. He decided that what he heard was not the rain on the roof, but the muffled roar of distant cannon. The armies of the Emperor Kang of Danova were attacking the fortifications on the Upalian frontier!

Teddy inhaled deeply and held his breath, his thin chest pressed against his sweat shirt. His Majesty King Theodore I of Upalia, resplendent in the black and gold uniform of a generalissimo, emerged on the balcony of his winter palace in Theodoresburg, capital of the Kingdom of Upalia. Through the square below rode squadrons of lancers, dragoons and hussars, batteries of horse artillery; behind them marched regiments of infantry. Grasping the diamond-studded hilt of his sword, King Theodore watched his army assemble to give battle to the enemy.

This would be the third war between Danova and Upalia. The first had been fought in the year 2032 and had ended in the defeat of the Emperor Kang and his imprisonment on the Isle of Hawks. But he had escaped through the treachery of Zikla, Duke of Anders, a general in the Upalian army, and in 2043 the Danovans had invaded Upalia a second time, aided by a renegade force under the command of Zikla. This time, they conquered Theodoresburg and massacred the population before being routed by King Theodore. On the day of victory, the Duke of Anders was brought to Theodoresburg and hanged in the city square.

The Emperor Kang was as evil and cunning as the Fu Manchu Teddy had read about in books. Now, astride a black war-horse, he directed his troops as they besieged Fort Lion on the Carian River. Hopelessly outnumbered, the defenders rallied behind their commander, Duke Lani of Caria, and prayed for the coming of King Theodore. . .

"Teddy!"

He sighed. This was his aunt, shouting from the foot of the stairs.

"Teddy!"

He opened the door. "Yeah?" he called sulkily.

"Come down here this minute and get ready for supper! How many times do I have to call you?"

"Okay, Okay. I'm comin'."

"— and be quick about it!"

"I'm comin', I told yuh."

His sneakers whacked the carpeted stairs.

She stood in the hall, a tall stooped woman with tired suspicious eyes.

"Seems to me you're spending a lot of time in that attic," she said. She wiped red, swollen hands on her apron. "You been into some mischief up there?"

He shrugged impatiently. "I ain't been doin' nothin —just playin'," he told her sullenly.

"Well, young man, you better wipe that scowl off your face and march to the bathroom and get ready for supper."

"Yes, ma'am," he enunciated carefully.

During supper, he was scarcely aware of what he ate; he was so deep in thought that his pork chop tasted no different than his whipped cream and jello. Mechanically, he obeyed his aunt when she told him to take smaller bites and to take his elbows off the table. He was pondering on the tactics that would have to be used by King Theodore in relieving the siege of the fort by the river.

If the Upalian army crossed the Tabelian Marshes, they might succeed in encircling the Danovans, but there was the risk that their cannon might founder in the morass. On the other hand, if they scaled the Purple Mountain. . .

"Look what you're doing, for heaven's sake!"

"Huh?"

His aunt glared at him. "Don't say 'huh' when you answer me. Look what you've done! You've spilled cream all over yourself."

He rubbed at his sweat shirt with a paper napkin.

"He's got his head in the clouds again." His uncle laughed mirthlessly. "Half the time, he doesn't know whether he's living on earth or Mars." Out of the corner of his eye, Teddy looked at his uncle's round, florid face and reflected upon his resemblance to Duke Zikla of Anders.

"Well, he'd better smarten up if knows what's good for him," his aunt grated.

"If he doesn't, I know something that *will* smarten him," his uncle said. He laughed again and reached for another helping of potatoes. Behind him, cloudy white marbles of rain slid down the window.

Suddenly, a cold shiver ran down Teddy's spine. What if the Danovans attacked Theodoresburg while the King and his army were on the way to the river. Old Kang was as cunning as a serpent. If. . .

"He spent most of the afternoon in the attic," his aunt said.

His uncle gave him a disdainful look. "He just about lives up there, doesn't he?"

"Yes, I think it's about time that one of us went up there and found out what he's been doing."

"No!" Teddy cried sharply.

His uncle laid down his knife and fork. "Look here, mister, I don't like your tone of voice. Have you been up to some of your monkeyshines up there?"

Teddy stared at his plate. "No," he said.

"Look at me when I speak to you. Have you been playing with matches up there?"

Teddy looked up. "No," he repeated. "I ain't been doin' nothin'."

"You'd better not be, if you want to be able to sit down for the rest of the week." The man resumed eating.

"After supper, I'll take a look to see what you *have* been doing," he said.

As his aunt gathered up the dishes, his uncle went into the living room and sat down in his easy chair to read his newspaper. Teddy sat by the window and looked out at the rain. The sodden grass of the lawn had turned a darker green and foaming rivers of rainwater ran down the street. He shut his eyes. Here there was no rumble of cannon, only the rain. He frowned and rested his chin in an upturned palm. Anyhow, the cannon were only playthings: scraps of cardboard held together with cellophane tape. What did it matter if his uncle saw them, or even destroyed them? But it did matter. Theodoresburg had been growing for a year and often it seemed more real to him than the town, the street and the home where he lived with his aunt and uncle.

"You'd better get at your homework. You won't get it done by sitting there staring out the window," his aunt told him.

"Yeah." He fetched his exercise books and spread them on the kitchen table. His aunt and uncle did not mean to be cruel, he knew. From time to time, by their acts and words, they showed that they were fond of him. Twice that summer his uncle had taken him trout fishing, and on both occasions there had been something subtly warm between them. And sometimes he detected a hint of affection in his aunt's voice even as she nagged him. But. . .

His uncle stood in the doorway between kitchen and living room, his shoulders shaking with laughter.

"You'd never guess what that kid has been doing up there!" He shook his head in wonder and amusement.

Teddy flushed and stiffened. His aunt turned from the sink where she was drying the last of the supper dishes.

"What's he been up to now?"

"You won't believe this, but that great big lummox has been playing with paper dolls."

"Paper dolls!" His aunt's laugh was dubious.

"They ain't paper dolls," Teddy mumbled. He pushed his chair back from the table and stood up.

"They looked like paper dolls to me. Paper dolls and doll houses. An eleven-year-old boy!" The man choked on his laughter. "The next thing we know, you'll be wanting us to put skirts on you!"

"I never heard of such a thing. Paper dolls!"

"They ain't dolls, I told you!" Teddy's fists were clenched, his arms stiff by his sides, his voice shaking.

His uncle pointed a warning finger. "Don't get sassy now, mister; I know paper dolls when I see them." Once again he burst into laughter. His cheeks were the colour of a tomato.

"Sit down and finish your homework, Teddy," his aunt said. Her voice contained a suggestion of weary sympathy. He resumed his seat and tried to focus on the blue lines in his exercise book. His uncle, still chuckling, returned to the living room and picked up his newspaper.

Paper dolls! His uncle had said that he should be dressed in skirts and hair-ribbons. And he could never explain. Theodore, King of Upalia, and his army — paper dolls! He slumped over the paper before him so that his aunt would think he was working. Yes, they *were* paper dolls. There was no King Theodore, no Emperor Kang, no Theodoresburg, no Upalia, no Danova. There was an attic full of preposterous cardboard buildings and ridiculous paper people.

It was still daylight when he finished his homework. The rain had stopped, but water still poured from the elms along the street. When Teddy went through the living room, his uncle did not speak, but he glanced up from his newspaper and grinned. The boy was blushing to the roots of his hair as he opened the hall door and started up the stairs.

The city was as he had left it. Yet everything had changed. Always before when he had come here, his flesh had tingled, his eyes had shone with excitement. Now there was only a taste like that of a spoiled nutmeat.

He bent and seized the cardboard palace. Gritting his teeth and grunting, he tore at its walls. The corrugated cardboard was sturdy; he was crying by the time he finished tearing it to shreds.

That night as he lay in bed, the memory of what he had done almost caused him to cry again. His earlier tears had been of frustration and rage. He had destroyed his city because he could not destroy his uncle. If he cried again it would be from grief. But he did not cry again. For something very strange happened to him: he became two persons.

One was the Teddy his aunt and uncle knew, the Teddy who now lay in bed and would get up in the morning and go to school. The other was a man in a black and gold uniform who carried a sword and rode a white horse. "The troops are waiting for your orders, Your Majesty," an officer said to him.

"Order the bugler to sound the charge," Teddy answered.

By the time that the Teddy who lay in bed fell asleep, King Theodore on his white horse had routed the hosts of the Emperor Kang and ridden in triumph through the gates of Fort Lion. Duke Lani had kissed his sovereign's hand while the people shouted, "Long live the King!" And, for the first time, he had met Duke Lani's daughter, the Lady Zorka, whose yellow hair hung down to her waist. . .

Every night after that, Teddy went back to his Kingdom. But, because it was invisible now, nobody ever knew.

# NIGHTMARE

*HE COULD HEAR* his father's voice calling him from the black kitchen at the end of the world. Resonant, edged with impatience. But he did not hear it from his bed, he heard it from a dark well in which he saw — actually saw, not just touched — the clammy stones with his fingers and cheeks, while his eyes inhabited another and incredibly distant place, a terrible courtyard full of beasts with wings like great scales, and these beasts had no names because no one but him had ever seen them.

It was as if his body had been dismembered and the pieces flung through the darkness, each piece retaining life and consciousness, his ears in one place, his eyes in

8

another, every separable unit of his body in a different place. A hideous, towering giant was loping across the world scattering pieces of his body like a man feeding hens by tearing hunks from a loaf of stale bread and hurling them down on his way across the henyard.

"Davie!" his father yelled. "Davie! For Crissakes git up. I gotta go ta work Davie. Davie!"

He wrenched himself awake with a titanic effort. The darkness of the room was thick as black wool. Morning was the fleece of a huge black sheep. He sat on the side of his bed and groped in the darkness as if he were trying to push the wool away from his face. His head burnt with a gritty dryness, as if dust had been poured into his skull through every orifice: eyes, ears, nostrils, mouth.

"Davie!" his father yelled again. "Davie!"

He stood up. The cold linoleum stung his bare feet, dust like sandpaper under his heels. He fumbled for his shirt and jeans, found his sneakers and walked into the kitchen in his shorts, groping through the unused room they called the dining room although he and his father ate all their meals in the kitchen, manoeuvring around the blacker bulk of tables and chairs, nudging the kitchen door open with his toes because his hands were full. He blinked in the sudden light, the sudden suffusion of heat, the sickening smell of hot grease, fried potatoes, bacon, and coffee.

"God, I thought you wasn't ever gonna wake up," his father complained. Huge as a spruce, dark and hard as a spruce, redolent of balsam, his father in his heavy red and black lumber jacket and leather-laced knee boots. "Look, your breakfast's on the stove. There ain't much wood in the stove. I didn't wanta leave a big fire in case you didn't git up. You'd bedder git dressed."

"Yeah, okay, thanks." He stood beside the woodstove to dress, sharp slivers of heat stinging his bare legs and back as he writhed into his shirt and jeans, stood on one leg to tie his sneaker.

"Bedder wear a coat ta school, I guess, hadn't ya?" His

father picked up his lunchpail and put on his cap. He went to the stove, carrying the lunchpail under his arm, lifted the cover and checked the fire. "I guess it'll be okay," he said. "Don't leave a big fire when ya go ta school." He turned toward the door. "We'll see ya," he said.

"Yeah, we'll see ya," Davie agreed. The cold denim chilled his legs and he backed closer to the stove, yawning.

His father gone, Davie found a clean plate and took a spoonful of fried potatoes and two strips of bacon. The bacon was moist and limp from soaking in the melted grease. He ate by the stove slumped in a chair, the plate on his lap. When he finished he carried the plate back to the table and poured himself a cup of hot coffee, splashing in canned milk until it had cooled enough for him to drink it all in three huge gulps. Then he poured water from the kettle into the tin wash basin in the sink and washed his face and hands, afterward patting cold water into his hair.

He was fully awake now and he felt better.

It was almost daylight and the electric light looked jaundiced and anemic in contrast to the clean sunlight arching through the dusty windows. He switched the light off and looked out through the glass. The sun had become an exploding furnace behind the bare, sinister maples at the other end of the Anthony pasture. A white shaft of smoke shot straight up from the rusty smoke-stack of the lumber mill north of the trees. The cover of a coffee can, used as an ash tray, sat on the window sill. He stirred the ashes with his forefinger, looking for a butt long enough to smoke. There wasn't any. His father was a frugal smoker.

The alarm clock ticking tinnily on the shelf over the pantry door told him it was seven o'clock. That meant he wouldn't have to go to school for almost two hours. Every morning he timed himself so he arrived at school just as the bell rang. That meant he'd be safe: all the other boys would be in their seats. There was no escape after school. Some of the boys always waited for him.

He'd start down the road, not seeing anybody, and trying to convince himself that perhaps this time they'd really gone home. He knew better. They hid in the ditches behind the alder bushes or concealed themselves behind the lumber piles above the mill. He'd read of a boy being chased by wolves. He understood what the boy felt, waiting for the wolves to leap, yelping from the bushes.

They surrounded him like wolves or Indians and there was nothing he could do about it. He was too shy to fight back. He shrunk down into himself like a puppy, shivering.

"Davie! Where's your mother! Ya-Ha! Davie!"

"Davie's mother's gone to the city to be a whore ain't she, Davie, ain't your mother gone to the city to be a whore, she's a bitch, Davie's mother is, ain't she Davie? Ain't your mother an old bag, a bitch and a whore, Davie? Ain't she gone to the city to be a whore? That's what my old lady says, Davie. You wouldn't call my old lady a liar would you Davie?"

"Damned sure he wouldn't. Answer him, Davie."

"I expect to git answered when I ask a man a question, Davie."

"Answer him, you yellow little bastard."

"Answer him you little son of a bitch."

"Answer him! Answer him ! Answer him!"

"My old lady says your goin' to the orphanage, Davie. How'd you like that? You think maybe your old bag'll come and take you out so you can go live with her in the whore house, Davie? You think so, huh, you think so, Davie, huh, you think so?"

"Answer him! Answer him! Answer him!"

"Ya-Ha! Davie! Ya-Ha! Davie! Ya-Ha! Davie!"

He went back to the sink and filled the basin with cold water, using a mug to dip it out of the water pail. He lowered his head quickly, covering his face. The shock cut off his breath and he jerked backward, shaking himself violently.

It was seven fifteen now.

He left the kitchen. Sunlight flooded the dining room but it was still cold. The slap of his sneakers on the cold floor made lonesome sounds in the room. He unhooked the door to the stairs and went through it, shutting it behind him. A cobweb broke across his face and he brushed it away nervously, climbing the stairs, breathing the odor of mustiness and abandonment.

He went into the bedroom that contained no furniture except a wooden framed bed with a spring but no mattress. Black clusters of swollen flies whirred insistently on the splotched glass of the single window. He shut the door and knelt by the bed, his knees clearing oval patches in the dust.

"I am David, the prophet of God," he said aloud. The harshness of his own voice in the empty room startled him. He looked over his shoulder, a little scared. He shook himself, angrily. "I am David, the prophet of God," he said again.

"Yes. Yes. Yes. David, the prophet of God," the room said. The voice of the room was remote but all-encompassing, like the hushed whistle of the night. "Yes, you are David, the prophet of God," it said.

"When I am a man I will remove mountains and hurl down the wicked from their high places and call down fire from heaven on the enemies of the Most High and my voice will silence the thunder and lightning will fly out of my fingers and the sea will part before me and there will be a great road that will open before me wherever I go even to the end of the world because I am David, the prophet of God," he said.

# LIAR, LIAR

*I HAD COME* into the house for a drink of water. "You kids," Aunt Lorna said as I dipped a white-enamelled pint mug into the water bucket. "I wish you'd either stay out or in." She was putting the top crust on an apple pie; having patted down the dough with her fingers, she began to trim it with a paring knife. The dark old farmhouse kitchen smelled of flour and cinnamon.

I emptied the mug and started toward the door. It was then I saw the white-faced, almost bald man in rimless eye-glasses sitting alone in the living room. "Didn't anybody ever tell you it's bad manners to stare?" Aunt Lorna said. "That's only your grandfather."

That stranger! It was very odd and a little disturbing that a man I had never seen before, not even in a picture, could be my grandfather. "I'm not staring," I said, turning the knob of the back door. Half-afraid she would make me go in to meet him and half-wanting her to do so, I wasn't sure whether I should dawdle or hurry.

"Don't slam the door behind you," she said, and then, turning toward the open living room doorway and raising her voice. "It's nobody, Dad. Just one of the kids."

I ran across the yard to the cow barn where my Williamson cousins and I were playing hide and seek. It was a cool September afternoon; the chokecherries had shrivelled or been eaten by the birds; velvety purplish cones hung from the branches of the sumac, and the rowan berries which only a few days before had been flaming orange were now the colour of rust.

I had known that my grandfather had come back after twenty years in Saskatchewan, "to die and go to hell," as my grandmother put it, "the Whoremaster!"

Now I had seen him for myself, and he did not look at all like any mental picture I had formed of him. "He was a ladies' man," I had heard my father say, "and one of the best damn teamsters in the eighteen counties of Nova Scotia. He wore a gold watch with a gold chain."

"The bugger could talk a hole through a cast iron pot," my grandmother had said, and once to torment her he had lit his cigar with a five dollar bill. He had worn a straw hat and spats, and he had played the accordion.

Then one fall he had gone west to help harvest the wheat crop, as thousands of easterners used to do, but unlike most of them he hadn't come home at the end of the season. He had left my grandmother with her three youngest daughters, and no one to help support them but a half-grown son.

"The chickens have come home to roost," she said when she heard he was sick. "Sure as there's a God in heaven it's the syphilis."

"We thought you must of fallen in," Allister greeted me, thinking I had been to the privy and making the stock joke. He was older and bigger than the rest of us and never allowed us to forget it.

"I saw him," I said. "Grandfather." I felt a little uncomfortable about applying that title to the white-faced old man. It sounded so ridiculous to me that I half-expected the others to laugh.

"So what," Allister said.

"Nothin'. I saw him, that's all."

"He reads all the time," Colin said. "Mum says she's scared he's goin' to turn into a Jehovah's Witness."

"He don't wear his teeth no more," Tinker said. "He keeps them upstairs. Beside his bed in a glass of water. They look funny."

"Granner, she says he's goin' to die," I said. At that time my grandmother lived with my parents.

"He's an old man," Allister said.

"He gave me a dime yesterday," Colin said. "I bought jellybeans and red licorice."

"Liar," Allister said. "Liar."

"Gramps has his own dishes to eat off of," Tinker said. "And his own knife and fork and spoon."

"Mum boils them," Colin said.

"That's to kill the germs," Allister said. "He's got TB."

I had heard more than enough. "Let's play, you guys," I said.

The best place to hide was the grain bin, because there was a darkness beyond the light like a cave behind a waterfall. The seeker crouched and looked into the bin, the light streaming over him, looked you in the face from five feet away and saw nothing but what he took to be a blank wall. Only I knew this. It was like being Invisible Scarlet O'Neil, or The Shadow.

Of course it was no fun if nobody thought to look. The fun lay in looking directly into the seeker's eyes without being seen. I didn't always hide there, because if you were always impossible to find the others might decide not to play.

What I remember best about that day was Colin tripping over a pitchfork and skinning his knee. At first we thought he was shamming to bring us out of our hiding places. He was howling his head off, hugging his hurt knee and jumping up and down on the other leg.

At last the three of us decided that he wasn't just pretending. By then he was seated on a block of pressed hay, swaying back and forth and sobbing.

Allister rolled up the leg of his jeans. "It ain't nothin'," he said. "Why, it's hardly bleedin' at all."

We had been a little frightened, and that made us a little angry. "You're nothin' but a crybaby," Allister said.

"Men don't cry," Tinker said.

"That's right," I said. "Men don't cry."

"Yes, they do," Colin said. "Gramps does. I've seen him."

"Liar," Allister said. But we all believed him.

# SKIPPER

SKIPPER WAS THE youngest of the five
sons of Ethel and Rupert Syverson. As a small boy,
Skipper, like each of his brothers before him, feared and
hated his father and entered into a wordless pact of
mutual defence with his mother.

Rupert, as he himself said, was a hard man. For sixty
hours in every week, he carried deal at the sawmill,
balancing the long, green boards on a leather-padded
shoulder and bearing them from the trimmer saw to the
lumber piles. Weeknights he lounged about the kitchen,
sluggish and sullen, until nine o'clock, then went to bed.
In his father's presence, Skipper adopted his formal

manners, as though before a stranger; he walked softly and seldom spoke. In conversation with his mother, Skipper spoke of "Rupert," never of "Father." For his part, Rupert demanded obedience but otherwise left his son pretty much alone. On Saturday night, like almost all of the mill hands, Rupert went to town and came home, violently drunk, at two or three o'clock the following morning.

When with his drinking companions, Rupert was sportive and exuberant. But when he came home drunk, he cursed his wife, called the boys brats and wished they were kittens so that he could sew them in a sack weighted down with rocks and drown them. On several occasions, he beat Ethel with his fists, and once he kicked her and sent her sprawling while Skipper stood by, screaming. Many times, he yanked Skipper out of bed in the dead of night and, on one pretext or another, flogged him with a cowhide strap. Often, if the weather was warm, Ethel led Skipper out into the night and they hid, wrapped in each other's arms, on the hillside overlooking the house until Ethel felt certain that Rupert's rage had been extinguished by sleep.

In a curiously dispassionate way, Skipper hated his father. He loathed the mill where Rupert worked himself into dumb exhaustion. He detested the men who came for his father with rum bottles hidden under their overall bibs. On numerous occasions between his sixth and his fourteenth year, he vowed to his mother that never, as long as he lived, would he taste strong drink.

Ethel fostered those aspects of Skipper's character which Rupert most despised. While a little lad in cotton shorts and a polo shirt, Skipper often brought her bouquets: handfuls of violets or bunches of mayflowers or daisies. She never took such gifts for granted; they touched her deeply, like presents from a lover.

She encouraged Skipper to daydream. She had done this with his brothers before him. When he grew up, she said, he would be a clean, sober man who would wear a white shirt and a necktie to work. He would go far away from the village and, of course, his mother would accompany him. Perhaps he would never become rich — but he would be a gentleman.

Skipper listened attentively to all that she told him. She was his guide and his refuge. A snivelling brat, Rupert called him when he saw him clinging to Ethel's skirts. His daydreams were foolishness, Rupert snorted. When Skipper grew up, he would go into the mill, as his father and grandfather had done before him. He would become hard, because a man had to be hard to survive. And if there was any man in him, when Saturday came he would get drunk, because the ability to drink was one of the measures of a man.

Skipper told his mother that he would die rather than allow this to happen to him. Often, at night, Ethel slipped into his room and lay on the bed beside him, and listened to him whisper of his thoughts, feelings and ambitions.

He liked to play with crayons. She bought him a water-colour set. To Rupert's vocal disgust, he spent many evenings making pictures at the kitchen table. On Ethel's infrequent visits to town, she bought him books. First, Hans Christian Andersen. Later, *Robinson Crusoe, Kidnapped* and *Treasure Island*. She rejoiced to see him run his fingers affectionately along the edges of the pages.

In Skipper, Ethel saw her last hope. His elder brothers had followed the old, brutal pattern to its conclusion. Harold, for example, had left school at fifteen to go into the mill. There he had learned to drink. At eighteen he got a girl in trouble and had to marry her. By the time he was twenty-two, they had four children. Ethel's daugher-in-law told her that now every Saturday night he came home roaring drunk like his father. The others, for whom she had once had such high and splendid hopes, were much like Harold. They were no different from any of the men who worked in the mill and lived in the village. Ethel's love for them had been soured by disappointment and hurt. Sometimes, thinking of what they had done with their lives, she almost hated them.

In the summer of his twelfth year, Skipper killed a sparrow with a sling-shot. Ethel looked upon this as an omen. To his astonishment, she wept and berated him. For several days, following this incident, she refused to speak to him.

For his fourteenth birthday, Rupert gave him a .22 calibre rifle. This gift, Ethel knew, had been inspired not by affection but by the knowledge that she would hate it. Sick at heart, she saw Skipper go hunting birds with his father. He came back dragging a partridge, a poor, bloody thing with dead, fear-crazed eyes. She could not bring herself to refuse to cook it, but she would not taste the meat. And she detested her son when she observed the gusto with which he attacked a greasy drumstick. "That Skipper's a dead shot for sure," Rupert boasted, eyeing his wife slyly. Skipper grinned, relishing his father's praise. For the first time, the man and the boy had established a bond of fellowship.

Still, she refused to believe that he would be like the others. It was not until the fall of his sixteenth year that she saw for certain what the future was destined to bring.

It was Saturday night. Skipper had gone to town with the boys, something he did frequently now. Most of these boys had left school and gone into the mill. Ethel harboured a dark suspicion that they were already learning to drink. She knew that they fought with their fists and picked up strange girls. She had warned Skipper about them. "Be careful, honey," she had said. He had patted her hand, reassuringly, and she had hated the amusement she detected in his eyes.

She was waiting up for him when he got home. Rupert had not come back from town. Ethel sat in the kitchen and listened to her son's movements in the porch. He was trying to be very quiet, she knew. The knowledge that she was going to surprise him gave her a strange sensation of triumph.

"Hi, Mama," he said as he opened the kitchen door. He wore his cap at a rakish angle, like the boys who worked in the mill. There were mud-stains on the sleeves of his jacket.

"Skipper. . ." She began.

"Yeah?" He continued to grin, swaying back and forth on his heels.

She got up from her chair and went over to him. She inhaled deeply, smelling his breath. Skipper laughed. "Yeah, Mama, I guess maybe I been drinking," he said.

She put her hands on his shoulders. "Skipper! You promised."

He shrugged. She had a momentary vision of him coming to her in his shorts and polo shirt, his hands filled with flowers.

"I'm a big boy now, Mama."

She returned to her chair and sat there, staring sightlessly at the floor. He shuffled his feet on the linoleum. "Look, Mama," he said. "I was talking to Bill Spence tonight."

Bill Spence was the foreman at the mill. *Don't say it,* she prayed silently. *Please don't say it.*

"He says he might be able to find a job for me."

"Yes." She would not argue. She would not try to reason with him. Already she had given up. For the fifth time, she had been defeated.

"We need the money, Mama."

"Yes."

"I didn't tell him yes and I didn't tell him no."

"No."

"Are you listening to me, Mama?"

"Yes."

He burst into laughter. "I just thought of something funny," he explained.

"What?"

"Oh, it doesn't matter." He laughed again. "The old

man really tied one on tonight. I ran into him in town. Drunk as a skunk."

In his voice, there was a strange alloy of contempt and empathy. Never before had she heard him use this tone of voice in speaking of his father.

Wearily, she rose and headed toward the stairs. "I'm going to bed now, Skipper."

"Okay, Mama. I guess I'll wait up for the old man." He threw himself into a chair at the table and lit a cigarette. For an instant, she hated him and wished that it were within her power to hurt him as he had hurt her. Then there was only the emptiness of defeat.

"You used to sit in that same chair and paint watercolours," she said.

He had not been listening. "Huh?" he said.

"Be careful of fire."

"Sure, Mama."

"Good night."

"Good night, Mama."

Ethel got into bed and switched off the light. In a little while she heard Rupert arrive. Then for a long time she lay in the darkness, listening to the man and his son laughing together at the other end of the house.

# GIRLS AND WOMEN,
# BOYS AND MEN

ZED, THE CAT, sniffed at the child's feet, a ritual he performed with every visitor. Was it mere habit, Tomlinson wondered, or a way of obtaining information? A cat's sense of smell was said to be thirty-two times as sensitive as a human being's. Did the animal file each new acquaintance according to scent, so that when this Stacey or Tracey returned to the apartment, he would recognize her from the unique chemical composition of her pubescent sweat and oils? "Hi, kitty," the girl said. Tomlinson grinned: she was obviously relieved to have somebody — anybody — other than him to talk with. Her fingers combed the furry white and black head. "Be careful," Tomlinson warned. "He scratches." Too late. There were red claw marks on her ankle. Zed stared at him in awesome feline complacency from beneath the chesterfield.

"I'm sorry," Tomlinson said. "Is it bad?"

"It's okay." Her smile was directed at the cat. She slipped out of her chair — she had been sitting in self-imposed discomfort a few inches from the edge of the seat ever since he had insisted that she wait for Mickey here rather than in the lobby — and knelt on the carpet. She unfastened her bracelet, a little silvery chain with tiny bells attached to some of the links, and dangled it just beyond the cat's reach. "It's safer to ignore him," Tomlinson told her.

Zed pounced. This time it was her wrist. He drew blood.

"Damn!" Tomlinson said. He stood up and looked for an instrument of punishment, chose *Time* magazine. But the cat had vanished.

The girl stuck out her tongue and licked at the blood. "Don't do that," Tomlinson said. "Here. Sit down on the footstool." He pushed it toward her with his foot. "Let's take a look." He examined her wrist. "Zed was only trying to be playful; the trouble is, he doesn't know how. It's Mickey's fault."

"Mickey?"

"Michael."

"Mickey!" Only a child could so jubilantly counterfeit incredulity.

"Let's see your foot." She extended it and he took it in his hands. "I feel like a shoe salesman," he said.

"What did Michael do to the cat?"

"When Zed was a kitten, Michael used to box with him. He'd put on a glove —"

"A boxing glove?"

"No. He didn't go quite so far as that. Just an ordinary glove. But it kept Zed from learning that people hurt when they get scratched." Her legs were the colour of a

Russet apple. He let go of her foot. "You'll live, Miss," he said.

"You've had Zed for an awfully long time then."

"Nine years."

"Nine years!"

He laughed. "In cat-years, he's forty-six years old. Even older than I am."

"Nine years ago, I was only a baby; nine years from now, I'll be twenty-three years old."

"Just to make sure you live that long, I'll get you some disinfectant for your wounds." She grimaced. "It's not as bad as all that," he said. She had told him her name; was it Stacey or was it Tracey? The girls of his generation had been Judys and Barbaras.

Predictably, Mickey hadn't cleaned the tub after taking his bath and had left his dirty clothes on the floor: jockey shorts, ankle socks, cut-off jeans and a T-shirt. The mess also included a comic book entitled *Conan the Barbarian*.

"Don't be silly, it's only rubbing alcohol," Tomlinson told the girl. She had clenched her teeth and shut her eyes as he took her wrist in his hands. He dabbed at the ugly red ladders with a bit of cotton. In contrast with her russet legs, her inner wrist was almost white. "Now the ankle. There's the good girl." He screwed the cap back on the bottle and dropped the bit of cotton in an ashtray.

"I'd better split."

"Let me buy you a Coke."

"No, thanks." The cat had reappeared and was washing himself, licking a paw and then wiping it across his face from eyes to jaw. "I love it when they do that," she said.

"You're sure you won't let me buy you a Coke?"

"Okay." She resumed her seat on the footstool, making that most female of all small, commonplace gestures: a sweep of the arm from hips to knees before sitting down in a skirt.

"Don't mess with Zed while I'm gone." In the kitchen,

he filled two glasses with ice and Coca-Cola, started back to the living room, hesitated, turned around, poured about half of the contents of one of the glasses down the sink and refilled it with Bacardi rum and a squirt of lemon juice. He was about to start out again when another thought struck him and he stopped to decorate the other glass with a slice of lemon and a cherry, and add a pair of candy-striped drinking straws.

"Cheers," he said. The rum tasted good. The girl kept very busy with her glass.

You never saw Russet apples in the supermarkets except at Christmas, when they appeared along with kumquats and chestnuts. When Tomlinson was a boy, there had usually been a crate of them in the basement. They tasted like wood-smoke and nutmeats and their flesh was so firm that after you ate one your gums ached.

The door-buzzer sounded. "It's about time," Tomlinson said. "Always forgets his key," he explained. Both of them stood up. "Excuse me while I admit the prodigal son."

"A guy stole my bike," Michael told them. "Don't blow your stack," he said to his father. "I got it back."

"Your cat scratched me," the girl said.

"He's not my cat."

"Your father told me how you used to tease him when he was a kitten."

"Dad!" Tomlinson was accustomed to one-syllable admonitions; but this time there was something else, something he had never before encountered in his son's voice, lips and eyes: the faintest hint of condescension.

"You should have phoned. You ought to show some consideration for your guests."

"What guests."

"Don't be a smart aleck," Tomlinson was about to say. He caught himself in time. "Forget it," he said instead.

Michael shrugged. Stacey or Tracey (or perhaps it was Leslie) had gone to him. "Thanks for the Coke," she said.

Tomlinson nodded. The young woman looked expectantly at the young man whom Tomlinson was seeing for the first time.

# THE
# PERSISTENCE OF
# THEODORE ROOSEVELT

*"HE'S BACK,"* WAS all that needed to be said. Theodore Roosevelt Bradgon had returned.

"Oh God. How did he manage it this time?"

"Got off the bus they'd put him on and hitchhiked back with some Yankee bear hunters. When Peter came home from work, the old guy was sitting on his front steps."

"Poor old bugger."

"Poor old Peter, you mean."

Everybody knew Theodore Roosevelt Bragdon. Or so he used to say when he came into the office of the Hainesville *Advertiser*, panting from the effort of climbing the front steps.

"You know me, boy?"

After the first time I could truthfully answer, "Yes."

"You're damn right you do. Everybody knows Theodore Roosevelt Bragdon!"

One of the first things I learned, working for the *Advertiser,* was that old men, Connaught County old men, expected you to know them even if they did not know you. To tell an old man who had lived in Connaught County all of his life that you did not know him was like telling him that his entire life had been in vain.

Of course Theodore Roosevelt Bragdon needed a slightly different kind of reassurance. He had been away for a long time and now he desperately wanted to come back. To accomplish this, he needed help; and where was help to be found if everyone had forgotten him?

Humpbacked with bulging eyes and a great gash of a mouth, he looked like a man-sized frog. There was always a cardboard box tied to his back with grocer's cord. Once the printing on the box read "Tawny Australian Port," and another time, "Red Devil Brand Canned Lobster, Salt Added." Sometimes there were labels that read "Fragile", or "This End Up."

The box had been tied to his back by the young guys at the railway station, partly so that he wouldn't lose it and partly because they thought it funny.

There were days when they made telephone calls for the old man, got him to lie down on a bench in the station waiting room, bought him a sandwich at Goldie's Diner, or even drove him to Peter's house. And there were days when there had been too much work or too little and they were either tired or bored, when they tied the box to his back and told him that there was a young guy at the *Advertiser* who would look after him. This was supposed to be a joke on me.

Their unthinking cruelty made me kinder than I might otherwise have been. As I helped the old man to a chair, telephoned Peter and talked with him until Peter came, I had the satisfaction of feeling superior to them.

He had been a white water man, working on the log drives on the St. John River. "Used to run back and forth across her, jumping from one log to another. Made a man feel like the Lord walking on the water." He had seen a man lynched in a British Columbia logging camp. He had been in San Francisco not long after the earthquake ("They had whorehouses there with Polynesian girls, Japanese girls, Chinese girls, you could find any colour of meat you liked") — in one San Francisco bar, he had shaken hands with James J. Jeffries, heavyweight champion of the world. He had sailed to India, Argentina, South Africa and Hong Kong. He had been in Vladivostok during the Russian Civil War with the Allied Expeditionary Force.

"We'd been there for months, see, and we hadn't seen no action. Everybody was always talking about the Bolsheviks, but we'd never seen one. Well, one day we was in this tavern, this pub, I don't know what they call them there, and there was this mouthy fellow with us — no, I'm getting ahead of my story. See, this pub was full of Russians. Crawling with them. And this mouthy fellow kept saying, 'Where's the Bolsheviks? Show me some Bolsheviks and I'll cut their hearts out with my bayonet,' he says. And, well, sir, this waiter comes over, this little Russian waiter, and he says real quiet-like he says, 'Sir, do you see that gentleman over there at the table by the door, that gentleman wearing the starched collar and the necktie?' And this mouthy fellow, he started to get to his feet. 'Is that one of them?' he says. 'Let me at him. I'll Bolshevik him all the way to hell.' I'm getting ahead of my story again. See, the reason this fellow at the other table was so easy to spot was he was the only fellow there who had on a suit and tie. So this little Russian waiter, he says, real quiet-like, 'No, no, sir, you misunderstand me; he is the only man in this room who is not a Bolshevik.' We wasn't long hitting the grit, I can tell you. I wish you could of seen the look on that mouthy fellow's face."

He seldom talked as coherently as this. Usually, getting sense out of his reminiscences was like trying to weed a garden without being sure which were the weeds and which were the vegetables.

"Hello, Uncle Teddy," Peter said, giving me a little bob of the head and a little half-shrug that meant, "Thanks, I'll do something for you in return sometime; but, God, I wish the old bugger wouldn't keep bringing outsiders into this."

"You know Theodore Roosevelt Bragdon, boy?"

"Sure, sure, Uncle Teddy. I'm Peter. Remember?"

That night or the following day, he would load the old man on a bus or train for Saint John, where someone from the Home was supposed to meet him.

A few times, he actually reached Saint John. But usually he got off at McAdam, if he was on a train, or at Woodstock, if he was on a bus. Once he got off before the bus got out of Hainesville.

Many old men and women search for the lost homes of their youth. One who I knew used to get lost on country roads in Nova Scotia, looking for the cottage in Scotland where he was born. I suppose he kept expecting to find it around the next turn in the road. The young have nightmares too, but theirs end when they wake up.

Theodore Roosevelt Bragdon was different. He did not search for an old home, but for a new one in an old place.

Hainesville was where he was born. He wanted to die there. But he had been away too long. His sons were in Michigan, California and New York. There was only Peter, who was not even his real nephew, but only a cousin so far removed that elsewhere he would not have been expected to know or acknowledge the relationship.

The old man was like one of those elephants my father used to tell me about when I was a child who walked the length of Africa to reach the only place where it was fitting for an elephant to die, except that Theodore

Roosevelt Bragdon was not so lucky as my father's elephants: he was always sent back to begin his journey again.

While in Hainesville, he would knock on the doors of large houses and ask to be taken in. "You've got plenty of room," he would say, "and I won't be around much longer." In some respects, the mad and the half-mad are more logical than the rest of us.

"The old fool should be locked up," said Mrs. Ransome, who kept the boarding-house where I lived. Many agreed with her. The others were harsher; they said, "So help me, if I was Peter, I'd poison him."

For a long time, I wondered how the inhabitants of Hainesville could be so pitiless toward Theodore Roosevelt Bragdon, Nathan the blind man, and Augusta Knight, the dishwasher in Goldie's Diner, who claimed to have nightly telephone converations with the Queen.

Eventually, I came to understand that it was because they could not help thinking of them as Theodore, Nathan and Augusta, rather than simply as an old man, a blind man and a mad woman.

Old or young, sick or well, as long as Theodore Roosevelt Bragdon lived, Hainesville would hold him responsible for being Theodore Roosevelt Bragdon, and there would be no escape from whatever rewards or penalties that might entail.

Mrs. Ransome had always believed him to be a fool, even when according to all accounts he was one of the most dashing young men in the County, and she saw no reason to revise her opinion now.

When I told her how I had driven off a gang of schoolboys who hooted in his face and mimicked his frog-like walk, then pelted him with snowballs, she only smiled grimly and remarked that it was the kind of devilment that he himself had delighted in when he was their age. "Now, he's finding out how it feels."

Yet, that spring when Theodore Roosevelt Bragdon,

who earlier that day had hitch-hiked back from Meductic some fifty miles away, breathed his last in Cockney 'arrison's pool room which also served as the Hainesville bus station, Mrs. Ransome put on her black hat and went to his funeral, as she always went to funerals she knew would be attended by few people other than the minister and the undertaker and the next-of-kin.

"Give the devil his due," she said to us that evening at the supper table. "When Theodore Roosevelt Bragdon set his mind on a thing he generally got what he wanted. I'll give him credit for that, the silly old fool."

# ONE COLD
# BRIGHT AFTERNOON

*A YOUNG MAN* is walking along a quiet residential street in a small town in eastern Canada. It is a cold, bright afternoon in early May and there are evening grosbeaks in the leafless branches of the trees and robins on the lawns covered with the winter's debris: beer bottles and doggy bones, a red and yellow mitten, a ballpoint pen, Kool and Player's cigarette packages, and numerous brown paper bags. The young man is twenty-five years old and it is important that we describe his appearance in some detail. In a little while, you will understand why it is important.

He has decided that he looks uncomfortably like King

34

Baudoin of Belgium, which is to say that he is too tall and too thin and wears glasses and has defenseless eyes but an obstinate mouth. His auburn hair is longer than is fashionable now in the 1950s; he has never worn a crew-cut because of the small bump at the back of his skull. There is a cleft in his chin and when he smiles at girls, which is not often, they usually smile back. His eyes are blue-gray (it pleases him that all the famous gun-fighters had blue-gray eyes) and there is a tiny mole about two inches in front of his right ear.

Fully clothed, he looks rather athletic, standing six feet, three inches tall and weighing one hundred and eighty pounds; but if he were naked, we would perceive that his chest is flat and there is a hint of fat around his middle. He wears moccasins and green corduroy trousers and a white turtleneck sweater which itches but obscures the scrawniness of his neck and the prominence of his Adam's apple. If he were talking, he would sound a little like Jimmy Stewart.

He has a respectable and increasingly depressing job at the local weekly newspaper, and has allowed himself to be elected secretary of the Junior Chamber of Commerce. He considers himself to be a very harmless person.

Two women walk about fifty feet in front of him. He has often seen and occasionally talked with them, for they are close friends of the woman who runs his boarding house and frequently one or both of them will drop in to gossip with her. The older and fatter one, who wears a hearing aid, is Mrs. Melanson; the slightly younger and thinner one, who talks incessantly in a very loud voice, is Mrs. Forsythe. Their husbands run small businesses.

He is thinking about a book that he finished reading less than an hour ago, the *Selected Letters* of John Keats, and of how when he came to the end, he said aloud, "Poor little red-haired bastard," and almost wept. He is also thinking of a girl with whom he went to a movie the previous Saturday night. Afterwards, he bought a six-pack of beer and a couple of Italian sandwiches and they parked on the road into a farmer's potato field. The moon was very big and bright and it felt very good to be young.

Mrs. Melanson and Mrs. Forsythe waddle onward, their bodies so neutered by the years that their lacy pink and blue hats look pitifully incongruous. They walk arm-in-arm and each of them carries a very large purse. If he had ever asked himself how he supposed they pictured him, he would have said, a nice, polite boy but shy, and it's a shame he doesn't get his hair cut and pay some attention to his clothes. There has never been any reason for him to ask himself such a question; he takes it for granted they regard him, as he regards them, with a vague benevolence.

When the two women reach Mrs. Melanson's house they stop to allow themselves to bring their conversation to an orderly and unhurried conclusion, and Kevin comes closer to them. Soon he is near enough to make out their words. Afflicted with the deafness that comes with age, they are unaware of this. He hears Mrs. Melanson say something about being afraid of somebody. Mrs. Forsythe laughs.

"I'm not joking," Mrs. Melanson says. "There's something about him that scares me."

"I can't think what it could be," Mrs. Forsythe says uneasily.

"There's something about his eyes," Mrs. Melanson says. "And the way he moves. Something that's not quite . . . right. He gives me the cold shivers."

Kevin has no choice but to continue walking toward them. The abruptness of their silence, now that they know that he is within earshot, almost unnerves him.

"Good afternoon," Mrs. Forsythe says, smiling more than is necessary.

"Good afternoon," Mrs. Melanson says.

"Good afternoon," he replies. His eyes avoid meeting

theirs. His cheeks are hot and he supposes they are red. "It's a beautiful spring day," he adds, almost desperately.

"Very beautiful," says Mrs. Melanson.

"Very beautiful indeed," agrees Mrs. Forsythe.

He wonders if they're expecting him to do some mad thing such as unzipper his trousers and expose himself. *The silly bitches*, he thinks. *Imagine anyone being afraid of me!* But he is not really angry, except at himself for being so absurdly ashamed.

# THE THIN RED LINE

*"IS HE REAL,* Daddy?" shrilled Terry-lene Cabana Set.

"We can't stop here; we're holding up the line," replied Air-Conditioned Forage Cap.

"Hurry up, Melissa; we haven't got any time to waste," added Drooping White Bermudas.

"But I want to know if he's real!" brayed Terrylene Cabana Set.

Richard stood at attention, as he had been taught to do as an Air Cadet in high school, in front of a sentry box inside the oak and iron doors of the blockhouse. Like all members of the Fort Clarence Guard, whether human or wax, he wore white duck breeches, a scarlet tunic with white cross-belts, and a hat like a bishop's mitre. A Brown Bess musket with fixed bayonet rested on his shoulder.

"I saw him blink!" whinnied Terrylene Cabana Set.

"Batteries," explained her mother, dabbing at her sweaty brow with a Kleenex. "They put batteries in them, and then set them so they'll blink every ten or fifteen seconds. I read about it in *Travel and Leisure.*"

"Nonsense," declared her father, who wore a T-shirt that read, *Where the hell is Conway, Texas?* "Limey soldiers have to stand like that. It's a tradition. The Thin Red Line. British Square. Stiff Upper Lip. All that Limey guff."

"For God's sake, let's go inside," said her mother. "The heat is killing me."

Was that a win or a loss? Richard wondered. At the beginning of the summer, it had depressed him that the tourists treated him as an object with no more identity, no more human feelings than a mound of cannon balls or the wooden shovels in the powder magazine. Now he played a game with them. The trick was to make them think he was just another of the wax mannequins they had been seeing ever since they checked in at the gatehouse. He took a malicious satisfaction in fooling them. Previously, he had been at their mercy; now he could pretend that they were at his.

"Don't be so damn neurotic," Sinclair had said to him. On the strength of being a Petty Officer in the Sea Cadets, Sinclair was being paid five dollars extra as Captain of the Guard. "Hurry along, folks," Richard heard him saying now, over the loudspeaker inside the blockhouse.

"— If you want to see some that really look real, you should see the ones in Madame Tussauds' in London," said Red-and-White-Checked-Shorts. "Of course, the chamber of horrors is a let-down. Been given too much of a build-up. The same as this place —."

"I'd like to steal that one and take him home with me," said Bikini-Panties-Under-Nylon-Stretchpants.

"Don't be so silly, Eleanor," Red-and-White-Checked-Shorts admonished her.

"Don't worry, Daddy," said Stretchpants. "He's probably neuter!"

"You watch your tongue, young lady," said Polaroid Swinger. Stretchpants giggled.

"I want him, Mummy! I want him!" Mustard, relish and ketchup on his face, Little Brother blatted.

"Oh, shut up, David," said Stretchpants.

"It's your fault, Eleanor; it was you and your foolishness that got him started," said Polaroid Swinger.

"Straighten up and fly right, you guys," said Red-and-White-Checked-Shorts.

Then they were all of them inside. Sinclair's electronically amplified voice came through the open doors. Richard wasn't certain how much of it he heard and how much of it he had unconsciously memorized and only thought that he heard.

"Old Fort Clarence was built in 1812 to defend the city against raids by American privateers. This is the last surviving blockhouse of this particular design in North America.

"Above, and to your right, you will see a portrait of Lord Holderness, its first commanding officer, who had the misfortune to lose his mind — his head got knocked off by a cannon ball." Here Sinclair paused, as Richard had known he would, and there was laughter.

"On the only occasion when the guns of old Fort Clarence were fired in anger, six members of the garrison died. None of them had suffered a serious wound during the fighting; but they weren't so lucky when they fell into the hands of the army surgeon." Again Sinclair paused and again there was laughter. "Now, follow me downstairs and I'll show you the dungeon."

"I like the ones inside better," said Terrylene Cabana Set when she came out. "They look realer."

"That's probably because this one is out where the sun gets at it," said Air-Conditioned Forage Cap.

"I still wish I could take it home with me," whinnied Stretchpants.

"Eleanor, don't get David started again, please," said Polaroid Swinger.

"Where to now, folks?" said Red-and-White-Checked-Shorts. "Will we go to the Indian Village or look for a place to eat? What will it be, redskins or Big Macs?"

Then, mercifully, they were gone, the last tour of the day. Richard went into the blockhouse to change his clothes.

"Have a beer," Sinclair said. He had taken off his scarlet tunic and sat, bare to the waist, on a bench between two mannequins.

"Thanks," Richard said. He too sat down on a bench, with a mannequin on either side of him. "There was this guy today that thought we were the British Grenadiers," he said.

"They're all jerks," Sinclair said, and took another drink of beer. "If they weren't jerks they wouldn't be visiting this stupid province."

"Yeah," Richard said. He began to remove his tunic. The faces of the mannequins, imported from London, had the broad noses and wide upper lips of the English working-class. "I suppose the guys that got killed had faces like that," he said.

"Huh? What are you talking about?" Sinclair said. He zipped up his jeans. "Who got killed?"

"I meant the guys that got killed here."

"Oh, them," Sinclair said. Having pulled on his T-shirt, he picked up his beer bottle.

"They were alive once," Richard said. "The same as you and me."

"Listen to the philosopher," Sinclair said. He finished his beer. "I'll see you tomorrow."

"Wait a minute," Richard said. "I'll go with you." Sinclair shrugged, but waited. Richard finished changing, hurriedly. He did not like to be left alone with the wax soldiers.

# CYNTHIA
## LOVES YOU

*THEY HAD BEEN* telling him for months that she loved him. Every night, before his mother and Dave had time to start yelling at him, he changed his shirt and washed the dirt from the potato house off his hands, then walked downtown to the drug store. If he had money, he bought a Chocolate Nut Sundae, so sweet it made his teeth ache. If he was broke, he squatted down at the rear of the store and looked at the comic books (he had once tried to make himself a Super Hero's costume of tights, mask and cape, but found he was too clumsy with a needle and thread; if it had not been for that clumsiness he might now have had a secret identity), or studied the glittering pictures of naked girls that made him fidget and sweat. There were always girls in the store, and when he looked up from the pictures and watched them he felt both frightened and triumphant, afraid that they would know what he was thinking yet feeling that his knowing how they looked without their clothes gave him a certain power over them.

There were boys in the store too. Some of them talked to him. No matter what he said, they laughed and nudged one another. Sometimes they bought him a soft drink or gave him a cigarette. Talking with the boys was the great event of the day. Especially when they told him the things the girl said about him.

" 'I'd like to wake up and find that Reade Morgan's shoes under my bed.' That's what she said, Reade. I heard her say it myself. She said she'd like to wake up and find Reade Morgan's shoes under her bed!"

That was Huff Fenwick, magnificent in his pearl-gray sports coat, puffing casually at a tailor-made cigarette. Reade knew that Huff understood how girls thought and felt. He was with them continually. Reade had watched him talking to them. The confident movement of his shoulders, the exciting, secretive little movements of his head.

Reade liked the idea of a girl being in love with him. He saw boys with girls everywhere. In the afternoons, in the pool room, the boys watched for girls. Girls walked by the huge, dirty window in swishing rainbow-coloured skirts or, if it was a hot day, they wore loose blouses and shorts. He liked to watch them too: the rhythmic rise and fall of their buttocks, the swing of their lithe, hairless, breakable-looking legs. The way the boys ran out after them from time to time excited him. A girl would go by, and a boy would put down his pool cue sheepishly while the other boys tittered. The boy and the girl might talk, outside on the pavement, the boy making vigorous motions and the girl replying with indecisive ones. Usually, they walked away together. It seemed to Reade that boys and girls were always walking away together.

He saw them on Saturday nights. At the beginning of the evening there were little knots of boys and little clusters of girls. Gradually, the two groups evaporated, until at last they had all formed pairs. Observing this process as he slumped on the drug store steps or leaned against a sign in front of the movie theatre (Double Bill Tonight Only: *I Shot Jesse James* and *Ma and Pa Kettle in Hawaii*), he felt his neck and ears burning, and hot little streams of sweat tickling his back and chest.

Girls were scared of him, he knew, and he thought this very foolish of them. He knew that he would never hurt them. He would handle them only with infinite tenderness. Their bodies looked so soft and vulnerable that he imagined they had to be touched with indescribable delicacy for fear of breaking them. He longed to touch a girl, simply touch her, letting his fingers glide down her cheek and across her neck or up and down her arm. But there were moments, sometimes, in which he believed that girls, for some mysterious reason, actually wanted to be hurt. At such times he wanted to jerk them down and slap them. He thought they might cry and beg for mercy, and he visualized the disarray of their clothes and the uncovering of the secret parts of their bodies. He moaned softly and clenched his fists, thinking about it.

There had been a hot, summer afternoon when he found a tiny, yellow-beaked bird, overcome by the heat, flopping in the dust behind the Knights of Pythias Hall. The bird's legs were spread far part and its yellow beak drooped, touching the ground. It trembled, shaking its slate-gray and buff-coloured feathers. There was the limpness of death about it. He enjoyed holding it in his hands and comforting it. Feeling its small body shiver in his palms, and watching its head shrink back as he stroked it with one finger, he felt sad that it could not fly. He wished he could make it well again. He crooned over the exhausted feathered thing, and lifted it up so that he could caress it with his cheek. But gradually his attitude changed. He became bored. He began to wonder what would happen if he pressed his hands together hard. He began increasing the pressure. The bird squeaked as he crushed it.

There was this same intermingling of tenderness and violence in his own body. There was his secret thing, for example, that could change so suddenly from a soft, reticent bud to a rod throbbing with impatience. It tormented and bewildered him, but it made him happy too. And he knew that the transformation was connected with the girls. There was magic in them, something invisible that flew out of their bodies and into his.

Cynthia Osler possessed such magic, certainly. He had sat on a stool at the drug store, eating a Pyramid Sundae, large scoops of chocolate, butterscotch and vanilla ice cream, and watched her as she stood at the magazine rack. Her hair was the colour of butterscotch sauce. She wore a white blouse and black shorts, and her bare arms and legs were tanned as brown as chocolate ice cream. He watched her scratching the back of her left ankle with the toe of her right sandal. Little muscles rippled in the backs of her legs. He shivered and felt as if he had eaten too much ice cream and was about to be sick. She was beautiful, so beautiful that he could hardly stand it.

And the boys assured him that she loved him.

He didn't believe them at first. But they swore it was true. She herself had told them, they said. He thought of all the exciting things he had seen boys do with girls, and of all the other things they did with girls when they weren't seen. Thinking of such things, he bit his tongue and a bead of saliva rolled out of the corner of his mouth and down his chin.

He saw boys drive through the streets in cars, their heads thrown back, laughing. Almost always, there were girls in the cars. Perhaps if he had a girl he would suddenly possess a car and know how to drive it; if one miracle occurred, why not another? His mother and Dave would stop yelling at him then. If he had a girl, he would get all the ice cream he could eat. Above all, a girl would help him to discover the source of the bottomless giddiness in his belly.

It was very late when she finished her work at the telephone office; the streets were deserted. It puzzled him that there could be so many people on the street in the daytime and none at all in the middle of the night. He often wondered where they all went. Thinking about it scared him. The dark scared him too, and he was afraid of the red waves of neon light that rolled across the black pavement, evaporated in the darkness and surged up again, still brilliantly red, only to evaporate once more, the process repeating itself over and over. He thought that Cynthia Osler must be frightened too.

Certainly she walked fast, not looking back, her arms swinging briskly by her sides, her heels clicking on the pavement. She crossed the street, coming toward him, and passed the mouth of the alley so that he saw her clearly. He wished that she were not wearing a trenchcoat; he wished that she were wearing the black shorts so that he could take courage from her chocolate legs. He knew she loved him. That had to mean she would want to show herself to him. Perhaps tonight she'll undress for me! he thought.

Reade stood up and walked to the mouth of the alley. She turned left at the corner and went out of sight. He started after her, stumbling as he tried to hurry. His heart pounded as though it were a bird inside his chest.

By the time he reached the corner, falling over his own feet, she had crossed the street again and was passing the barber shop. Here the street lights were higher and farther apart. There were no neon signs. But she was less than two hundred feet away and he could see her clearly;

the swing of her arms, the slight bob of her head, the brisk back and forth rhythm of her trenchcoat and the liquid up and down rhythm of her buttocks. If she looked back, she would see him. He was tempted to call to her. If he called her name, she would turn and perhaps run back to meet him.

The thought made his stomach turn over. But he wanted to surprise her. He made as little noise as possible, crossing the street.

He was close to her now. He decided to surprise her in the alley between the railway station and the freight shed. It was dark there and he could kiss her, because there would be no chance at all of their being seen. It would be nice to have someone watch, envying him, when she let him kiss her. But he was afraid that would make her shy. He wanted her to undress for him.

He remembered her legs in the black shorts. They were covered with a yellow fuzz like the hair on peaches. Tiny beads of moisture clung to the fuzz. And the muscles rippled like water under her chocolate skin. Remembering, he moaned and walked faster.

Then he started to run, headlong like a child, chin down and arms flailing. Turning into the blind darkness of the alley, he scraped against a sharp corner of the railway station wall. He heard his coat rip and felt a stab of pain. He ignored it. Even before his eyes became accustomed to the darkness, he knew that she had stopped in the alley and was standing there, waiting for him. Her heels had stopped clicking. As he halted, he heard nothing but the wind of his own breath.

He saw her. Her back was pressed against the wall of the freight shed, opposite him. Her eyes were very wide and her mouth was half-open. Her arms were raised, elbows extended, her hands level with her face. The arms looked like wings, he thought, like the wings of a bird.

He laughed and went over to her, intending to touch her gently, wishing she would speak to him.

# THE INSURANCE MAN

*THE IMPORTANT THINGS* to bear in mind about Pegiel Tucker are that he was in the insurance business and his roots were in Rumford, New Brunswick.

Rumford is a little place. At any given moment, almost every adult in town will be able to tell you the exact population. Ask how large it is and you will be told that it was 2,017 at the last census, but since then eight people have moved in and twelve have moved away. Just about everyone in Rumford prides himself on his knowledge of local demographics. There is even a game which consists of counting the resident widows. If a group of Rumford women get together to quilt a quilt or a group of Rumford men stay after Lodge to play Auction 45s they're likely to end up counting widows, starting with the eldest, Mrs. Doctor-MacGuire, widow of The Old Doc.

"It's hard to believe how many widows there are in this little town," somebody says.

"Let's count them," somebody else says. "Just for the fun of it." The game begins.

Small places have their own distinct personalities, just as small people do. Rumford is as different from the neighbouring towns as New York or London or Toronto is different from other cities. In fact, Rumford has a stronger identity than any large city. The identities of large cities are essentially mythical, the creation of artists and historians, whereas the identity of Rumford stems from a people with the same origins having lived in close association in the same spot for a long time: it's very real.

There was a Pegiel Tucker in Rumford as far back as 1785. He had fought with the King's American Dragoons, under the Count Rumford, in the American War of Independence. His youngest son, Abram, founded the Reprieved Baptist Church, the Tuckerites. It is a dwindling denomination, partly because it teaches that clergymen ought not to receive salaries, but there is still a Reprieved Baptist Church in Rumford. The modern Pegiel Tucker sent it regular donations during his thirty years in the insurance business in Chicago.

This Pegiel went to Chicago as a very young man, at an age when today's young men are called kids and, to the astonishment of Pegiel's generation, even think of themselves as such. There was a time when everybody in Rumford had a brother or an uncle in Chicago. There is actually a spot in Chicago called Rumford Corner, just as there is a Rumford in Zimbabwe, so named by the Rumford-born missionaries who founded it as a mission station. (There was a Rumford man, the son of one of those missionaries, in the old Rhodesian Parliament.)

Up until a few years ago, the Rumford *Free Press* mailed one hundred or more copies a week to Chicago addresses and each year carried an advertisement for the annual Chicago Rumford Picnic (no liquor allowed).

Like many of those young men who went to Chicago, Pegiel Tucker came home one summer, married a Rumford girl, and took her back with him. And, like most of those married couples, the Tuckers kept coming back to Rumford. At first, it was every third or fourth year. Then, as they became more prosperous, it was every second year (and practically all of them prospered to some degree). They brought their children with them when the children were young; later the children preferred to go to camp back home, by which they meant Illinois: when their parents said back home, they meant Rumford. A few of the children came back once or twice to Rumford after they had grown up. Young deerhunters with strange accents whose wives slept in until noon and said "Oh, Christ" and "Darling."

Unlike the others, Pegiel eventually came back home to stay. He brought with him his wife's corpse, to be buried in the Tuckerite Graveyard, bought a house, hired a housekeeper, and resumed conversations that had been interrupted by his departure thirty years before.

He became one of the regulars at Diaper Kelly's barber shop. (Diaper had acquired his nickname as a result of his habit of singing to himself, "di-dee, di-dee, di-dough," as he worked on a customer's head or face.) Diaper's place was one of Rumford's men's clubs, the others being Perley's Irving Station, Hank's Radio-TV and Cockney Harrison's pool room. Two or three times a week, Pegiel spent an entire evening at Diaper's, smoking cigars and discussing harness racing, baseball, hockey, or trout and salmon fishing. He dressed a little more informally than other Rumford men of his age, favouring a polo shirt and a baseball cap, and smoked a more expensive brand of cigar. Occasionally, he used a figure of speech with which they were unfamiliar. He was credited with the ability to grasp the impossible complexities of the U.S. electoral system. But there was no doubt in anybody's mind that he was a Rumford man, that he belonged.

Like the others who gathered in the barber shop (which Diaper finally had to close down when there was nobody left in the world who wanted a short back and sides with a little off the top), Tucker spoke in praise of hard work, iron thrift and all the other horrible necessities which they had faced in their youth and been able to endure only by convincing themselves that they were Christian virtues. Not surprisingly, he was especially vehement about the value of insurance. He often said — and no matter how often he said this, it was with the air of a man announcing a great breakthrough in human thought — that a man who was under-insured was a fool.

He had learned his lesson the hard way, he said, and his companions grunted or nodded to affirm that the hard way was the best way. Before he got into the insurance business, he had owned a store, a little corner store that sold sodas, candy, tobacco, magazines and newspapers. Not much, maybe, but not all that bad either, for a guy who had arrived in Chicago with the seat out of his pants. He had been driven out of business by the neighbourhood hoodlums. And they weren't spades either, he added. Chicago was a rough town in those days; Chicago was still a rough town.

There had been no insurance. You didn't need that kind of insurance where he came from, insurance against vandalism and theft. He was ruined. Right back where he had started, with the seat out of his pants. And then he had an idea. The best idea he had ever had in his life. He started to sell insurance. Theft and vandalism insurance. His sales pitch consisted in giving potential clients an account of what had happened to him and could as easily happen to them. He acquired a partner — a spaghetti-eater, but not such a bad guy for a spaghetti-eater. Before very long he had men working for him. A good many of them were Rumford men. He never asked any of them to do anything that he wouldn't do himself. He paid them well and expected a dollar's work for a dollar's wage. And — to make a long story short — here he was today, not Rockefeller or K.C. Irving, but able to afford all the creature comforts, including fifty-cent cigars.

A few months after Pegiel Tucker died in his sleep and was buried beside his wife in the Tuckerite Graveyard, there was a little story in the New York *Daily News*. One of those flashback items. It recalled that in Al Capone's heyday the man in charge of his protection racket was one Pegiel Tucker, who had recently died in Canada. Somebody picked up a copy of the paper in Fredericton and it was passed around Rumford. Nobody was shocked. They had always known that he was in the insurance business. That is how they looked at it. But the fascinating thing about all this is that Pegiel himself had looked at it that way too.

# HELLO
# OUT THERE

*IT COULDN'T HAPPEN* now, not with computers, microwave networks and direct distance dialling. This occurred in the olden days, about twenty years ago, when I lived in a small town where there were telephone operators who knew everybody.

You'd be paged at the movies, and when you reported to the lobby the ticket-seller would hand you a telephone and it would be a long distance call from someone who had tried to reach you at home and was told by the operator, "He's not there; on my way to work, I saw him going into the theatre — I'll try there."

That was fine, except when you didn't want to talk

with anyone, and maybe had gone to the movies in hope of avoiding this very call.

If she was convinced you were at home, the operator might keep your telephone ringing almost indefinitely. Once, after the person at the other end of the line told her it was important, she even called the family next door and had them send over their young son to see what was the matter.

This meant that the doorbell began ringing too, while I sat on my bed upstairs, cursing everyone who refused to leave me in peace.

Then, in the traditional manner of small towns, the neighbours' boy entered the kitchen, calling, "Is anybody home? Is anybody home?"

I took off my shoes and tip-toed to the door of my room, so that if he came upstairs I could hold it shut against him, without letting him know I was there. But, after a while, he went away.

One of the operators — her name was Dorothy but everyone called her Doe — got it into her head when I first came to town that my name was Robert. In the beginning, I didn't correct her, because in those days I hated to disappoint people: it made me feel as though I had let them down somehow, failed to live up to their expectations. I know that's absurd; but that's how it was.

Besides, I liked the way she said it, *Robert,* as if she enjoyed the way her mouth and throat felt when she enunciated it. Later we would both of us have felt uncomfortable if she had called me by my right name.

I was so young then that if there was a risk of my overhearing my acquaintances talk about me, when I was in an adjacent room for instance and they didn't know it, I would either cough loudly to warn them or, sometimes, if I was in the bathroom, actually put my hands over my ears.

Doe had never married, but she wasn't the conventional small town spinster. She had a grown daughter by one man and spent her weekends with another, an alcoholic veteran, one of those soldiers who never really came back from the war.

I talked with her occasionally during a coffee break at one of the town's two restaurants: a big-boned, mare-hipped woman with natural red hair, drinking hot chocolate topped with a toasted marshmallow or smoking a mentholated cigarette. And once in a while, when I felt a certain kind of loneliness, I would telephone her, always from the office and always late at night.

I worked for a weekly newspaper and lived in a boarding house, so I spent a good deal of time in the office outside of working hours, doing odds and ends of things, or just being alone. The people I knew, I knew too well, so that none of them ever surprised me and, worse, I had got into the habit of not surprising them.

I'd walk the length of Main Street, selling advertisements and picking up bits of news, and presenting a slightly different persona to everyone I met. Everyone I met knew a different Kevin O'Brien, and none of them was me. Nor was Doe the only person who knew me by a name that wasn't mine; the manager of one of the grocery stores called me "Kenneth."

The offices of the weekly newspaper consisted of two small and dusty rooms at the front of the building, crammed with desks, old L.C. Smith typewriters, filing cabinets, stacks of back issues, and cardboard boxes containing completed jobwork.

The rest of the first floor was a single large room, the printing shop, and at night, through a doorway, the light from the office faintly illuminated the almost frighteningly silent and motionless perforator, paper cutter, stapler, presses, and linotype machines. There is something eerie about a plant that is not in operation, especially at night, and more especially if you've worked there.

This was an old building. On Sunday afternoons in the winter there was often a poker game in the basement. In the small hours of the morning, young pressmen and their girls had made love on the long tables in the printing shop. The founder of the paper was said to have died in the swivel chair in which I sat as I snapped off the cap of a bottle of beer and turned the crank of the old-fashioned telephone.

As I've said, I called Doe only when I felt a certain kind of loneliness. The beer wasn't meant to dispel that loneliness but to nurture it; after three pints object and emotion were so softened that they flowed together and became all but indistinguishable. It's great to get quietly and moderately drunk when you're very young and drunkenness is still a new country to be explored. Later you learn that drunkenness is like dreaming of the enchanted cavern in a fairy tale: a place where you discover a great many priceless things, none of which you ever succeed in bringing back with you.

Only one operator worked after midnight, and there weren't enough calls to keep her busy. So Doe and I could talk as long as we liked. If the line went dead, that meant she was handling a call; and I waited, my head cocked to one side so that the telephone was held between my cheek and shoulder, until she came back on the line.

Not that I ever spent much time talking with Doe, although I've no doubt that she did a considerable amount of eavesdropping on the calls that she put through for me to operators in other little towns all over Canada and the United States.

For that was the game. It began one night when I tried to reach a friend in Montreal and there was no answer. "You sound lonesome," Doe said. And I wanted to say, "It's none of your damn business," because back then I was ashamed of being unhappy. "Do you want to talk to somebody?" she said. "Why not," I said, thinking she meant I could talk with her. But a minute or two later I was talking with a girl working a switchboard in Newfoundland. She had an Irish-sounding accent. We must have talked for an hour or more. Every fifteen minutes or so she'd have to answer the switchboard, and during the interval of silence I'd light another cigarette or take another drink of beer. We said all sorts of silly things to each other.

Later that night I talked with operators in Manitoba, Nevada and Idaho; or perhaps they were in Montana, Arizona and Saskatchewan; it doesn't matter. They were all of them young and lonely and not very bright small town girls who read movie magazines and wanted to look like Piper Laurie. But that sounds condescending, it wasn't that way at all. Hell, it pleased me that Marshall Thompson in the movies — does anyone else remember Marshall Thompson, I wonder? — was the same height and weight as I was, six feet three inches and one hundred and forty-six pounds; and tears came to my eyes during that scene in *The Gunfighter* where Gregory Peck's little son goes to his father's funeral — all through the film he has been kept from knowing that he is Gregory Peck's son because Peck is a gunfighter — and he says to them at the door, "Let me in; I'm Jimmy Ringo's boy."

I spent at least a half-dozen nights like that during the following twelve months. Sometimes I was on the telephone from midnight until dawn, and I must have talked with more than fifty girls at one time or another. I can still recall the names of a few of those disembodied voices: Norma, Helen, Joyce, Louise. We had long conversations too, but I don't remember anything that was said; even at the time what was said didn't seem important, it was the saying that mattered.

A few of the girls, a very few, lived within easy driving distance and occasionally I told one of them I'd come to see her, and sometimes I meant it, or thought that I did. But I didn't really want to meet them; I wanted them to remain as they were, unknown and unknowable. It was the mystery of them that pleased me.

It was almost beside the point that they were female,

except insofar as their being female made it easier to pretend that we were observing certain social conventions, rather than an almost mystical (that's no exaggeration) experience with someone who was not only a stranger but almost certain to remain so.

It didn't always work, and some times were better than others, but at best we didn't so much converse as prattle like young lovers who lie in each other's arms, each of them crooning words that the other needn't pretend to comprehend, because the words aren't part of a message, but only another kind of touching.

# WILL
# YE LET
# THE MUMMERS
# IN ?

*CLAYTON MURDOCH, OWNER* of the old Peabody place, awoke, stretched, and felt that life was good. Then he got out of bed, pulled on wool socks, and went to the window, flexing his arm muscles like a boxer. His world, this morning of the twenty-fourth of December, was a monochrome in bluish white. "What time is it?" Barbara said.

With her auburn hair spilling over the shoulders of her long-sleeved nightdress, she looked quite the proper mistress for this one hundred and fifty-year-old house. "I didn't mean to wake you," he said. "It's five to eight." He looked out the window again. Bluish white fields, bluish white fences, bluish white trees, and in the distance two bluish white houses under a bluish white sky. "The silence," he said, inhaling the wonder of it.

"I don't notice it as much as I did in the summer," Barbara said. "The birds made just enough noise to remind you that noise existed. I miss the birds." From the hen-house, as if on cue, there came the muffled crowing of the rooster they had named Frank Harris. "Not you, stupid; the real birds."

"We'll get some records," Clayton said. "The next time we're in Toronto. Birdsong records. So that next spring we'll be able to identify them." He pulled on his Aran Islands sweater over his pajamas. Would it be cheating, he wondered, to buy an electric heater for their bedroom?

"Crows caw in units of three," Barbara said. "Caw. Caw. Caw." She inhaled. "Caw. Caw. Caw. Mrs. Perley told me. She also told me that crows hold trials. They form a circle on the ground, she said, with the crow that's been accused of a crime in the centre of it; and if they find him guilty they kill him. Her father had seen places where the crows had held court, she said. There'd be a dead crow lying there with a circle of crow tracks around it."

"That's terrific. I must ask Bob Warren in the folklore department about it."

"I'd rather you didn't."

"Why not?"

"We came here to live, remember? Not to research a dissertation on the quaint beliefs and practices of the natives."

"Purist." He touched his index finger to his lips and then to the tip of her nose. "What would you like for breakfast? I'd suggest one of Murdoch's famous omelettes."

"I'm going to be shamelessly decadent and go back to sleep. Tonight could be hectic and God knows at what unholy hour Barry will get up tomorrow."

"I think I'll take the VW into town as soon as I've had breakfast," he told her. "Collect food and drink for the multitudes."

"For the Mummers," she said. "The Mummers." She frowned, pushing out her lower lip with the tip of her tongue. "Mummers. Mummers. After you say it aloud a few times it starts to sound sinister."

He plugged in his razor; there was no outlet in the bathroom. "Any word will sound sinister if you keep repeating it. Didn't you ever frighten yourself that way when you were a kid? I did. I'd pick a word, and say it over and over again until I almost wet my pants, I was so scared." The razor clicked and went dead. "Damn. I've blown another fuse. We're going to have to hire an electrician to go over this place from top to bottom."

"Why don't you let it grow? You looked like a nineteenth-century Russian nihilist when I met you."

"And have everyone in Butler's crossing refer to me as that bearded weirdie professor? No, thanks." His hand was on the brass doorknob. "I'll shave in the kitchen. Like a good farmer. And don't worry about tonight. Everything will be fine."

"I'll stay here with six good men while you take the buckboard to town."

"A whole squadron would never get through, but one man flying low might make it."

She blew him a kiss.

To reach the stairs, it was necessary for him to pass through his son's room. Several of the oldest houses in Butler's Crossing, erected by men who had fought with Butler's Rangers on the losing side in the American War of Independence, were built with some of the upstairs rooms situated behind the others and without direct access to the hall. According to local legend, the object was to ensure that nubile daughters were unable to leave the house at night without waking their parents; but

Clayton surmised that it was actually a matter of obtaining the maximum benefit from the available heat.

Barry slept in his Snoopy and the Red Baron pajamas, beautiful and squalid, a golden angel with snot on its upper lip. He'd have room to grow here, where there were birches for him to swing on, and a swimming hole where he had gone skinny-dipping last summer. (The boy had been very self-conscious at first, it was so strange to strip naked outdoors and swim among darting fish). Next year, Clayton decided, I'll buy him a horse. He smiled at the thought of the heir of the lower middle class Murdochs riding a horse like the Queen of England's daughter.

The kitchen, larger than many apartments he had known, smelled of mint and dried apples. Through the window, across the bluish white fields, could be seen the orchard where the apples had been picked, he and his wife and son working together, "like the old pioneers," Barry had said. Nearer the house were the chokecherry bushes from which they had gathered berries — "We must be careful to leave enough for the birds," Barbara had kept saying — to be made into a thick, sweet wine. In the living room stood the ten-foot-tall spruce he had chopped down and they had dragged home to be decorated with red and green paper streamers, Christmas cards and popcorn balls.

Into a bowl he broke three eggs that had been laid the previous day by his own hens, brown eggs in memory of his postgraduate years in England. He stirred in three tablespoonfuls of water from his own well, white pepper, a pinch of sea salt and two heaping tablespoonfuls of grated Cheddar, made locally and sold at the weekly Farmers' Market in town. Two slices of homemade bread, containing stone-ground wheat, an orange and a glass of milk completed his meal, after which he took his Vitamin C, Vitamin E and halibut liver oil capsules.

Barry was up. Yawning and blinking, his eyes slightly out of focus, his body and mind undergoing a child's long slow ascent from sleep to wakefulness. "Hiyuh, guy," Clayton greeted him. "Want the old man to whip you up an omelette?"

"I'd rather have a cheeseburger," the boy said.

Clayton laughed. "You're a barbarian, do you know that?"

"What's a barbarian?"

"A barbarian is someone who eats cheeseburgers for breakfast and doesn't use his handkerchief."

"I wasn't picking my nose. I was scratching it."

"Okay. But next time use a handkerchief. How about an enormous bowl of Granola and a tall glass of fresh milk from Carvell Perley's Jersey cow, unpasteurized and free of all chemical additives? There's a civilized breakfast, my son."

"Gary Armstrong picks his nose all the time," Barry said. "He's the toughest guy in Butler's Crossing."

"What makes you think that?"

"He put a guy in the hospital."

"Somebody's been kidding you."

"I was there."

"You were there?"

"Sure. All the kids were there." The boy shadow-boxed. "Wham! Gary gave it to him right in the mouth. And then, wham! he gave it to him again, right in the guts. And when he got him down he kicked him. There was blood all over the place."

"Sounds to me as if you'd been watching too much television again."

"I didn't make it up. Ask anybody. Ask Bud at the diner. That's where it happened: in the yard out back."

"Are you sure you aren't exaggerating, just a little?"

"I am not exaggerating. There was blood all over the place, just like I said."

"And when did all this happen?"

"Yesterday afternoon."

"How come you didn't mention it before?"

The boy shrugged. "I don't know. Just never thought of it, I guess."

"Drink your milk."

Barry drank. "The other guy was an Indian," he said.

Oh, Lord. "Do you think that made it right?"

"Do I think what made it right?"

"Do you think it was all right for Gary Armstrong to beat up a guy just because he was an Indian?"

"No."

"Listen, guy, I want to have a talk about this with you. Later. In the meantime, let's not say anything about this to your mother. Okay?"

"Okay." Barry finished his milk and wiped his mouth on his sleeve. "I bet Gary Armstrong eats cheeseburgers for breakfast," he said.

On the way to town, Clayton listened to the news on the car radio. Killing in Ulster. Killing in Lebanon. Killing in Angola. Killing in Eritrea. Killing in Timor. Where was Timor? The planet was a house packed with children whose parents had abandoned them. When the children were not destroying furniture or smashing windows they were at one another's throats. One day they would set the house on fire and that would be the end of it, and of them.

Back in Chicago, a neighbour of the Murdochs, the wife of a professor, had been beaten to death in her own apartment by a boy of Gary Armstrong's age: fifteen. But that was in Chicago (Shy-Cargo, they pronounced it here). There hadn't been a murder in Butler's Crossing since the 1920s. He was aware of this because people still talked about it. A MacKinnon boy had killed his girl-friend, and been hanged for it. They were both of them buried beside the Baptist Church.

He stopped at Munroe's Texaco for gasoline. Graham Munroe came out to the pumps, a fat man in a black overcoat; Graham's Kosygin coat, Barbara called it. "Morning, Professor," he said. "A great day for tracking deer, eh?" This was hunting country. The locals killed deer and moose; Clayton could make large allowances for that — unlike Barbara who had at first refused to cook the venison steak that Graham had given them that fall — but he shared her detestation of the business executives from New York and New Jersey who flew up in their private planes to get drunk, play poker and shoot bears.

"Would you fill it up, please, Graham?" Clayton got out, as customary in Butler's Crossing, to stand and talk with the man working the pump. "How is Florence?"

"Able to sit up and take a little nourishment." This was one of the standard local responses to such a question, an old joke. As Clayton knew, Florence Munroe was in the best of health. "How are all your folks?"

"Just fine, Graham. We're all looking forward to tonight."

"To being visited by the Mummers, you mean?" The big man returned the hose to its hanger. "It's mostly foolishness. Just a bunch of the fellows letting off steam." He glanced at the gauge on the pump. "That will be $9.75, Professor."

Clayton accompanied Graham inside, so that he would not have to come back with the change. The counter held display cards of Alka-Seltzer and of Gillette, Wilkinson and Schick razor blades. "You're becoming kind of a celebrity around here," Graham said as he punched keys on an ancient cash register.

"A celebrity?"

"Everybody's talking about your Committee."

"Oh, that. It's not my Committee. I'm just a member. And not a very active one. I just happen to believe that it would be a bloody shame to let a pulp company pollute this valley. If they're not stopped, no one will be able to fish or swim in the river — not to mention the fact that the pulp mills stink to high heaven."

"Some folks call that the smell of money," Graham chuckled. "Hey, I almost forgot. The wife would of killed me if I hadn't given you this." He reached under the counter and came up with a package wrapped in tin-foil. "It's one of her year-old fruit cakes. She wanted you people to have it."

"I don't know what to say." Clayton pulled back a corner of the tin-foil. "My God, but it smells good." The aroma of cloves, cinnamon, raisins, currants and brandy momentarily enveloped his mind. "Thank you, Graham, and give Florence a kiss for me."

Afterwards he wondered if that had been the right thing to say and decided that it probably hadn't been. In Butler's Crossing, certain formalities were involved in every relationship, including the most intimate ones; even the closest friends, even husbands and wives, kept a little distance between one another, always. Theirs was the better way, Clayton suspected, but it was too late in his life for him to learn to be comfortable with it. If the old girl had been there he might actually have given her a peck on the cheek before he thought — and what an embarrassment that would have been for all three of them!

The road was a trifle slippery, with powdered snow, and in the tree-shaded stretches there were patches of ice, but he had it largely to himself. Driving the twenty miles to town, he met or passed only six or seven vehicles. Most of the drivers blew their horns, flashed their headlights on and off or waved.

He picked up his mail at the university. Invitations to New Year's parties, memos from the chairman of the department, Christmas cards from Chicago, Toronto and London, a letter accepting a paper on D. H. Lawrence's influence on George Orwell that he had submitted to

*Queen's Quarterly*, and a note from Bob Warren reminding him that they had agreed to have lunch together today at the Faculty Club.

The campus was deserted except for the few foreign students who had nowhere to go for the holidays. Next year, he resolved, he and Barbara would fill the old house with young Taiwanese and Pakistanis, give them a real old Cornelius Krieghoff kind of Christmas. Perhaps they would also invite some of their Butler's Crossing neighbours, the Perleys, Munroes, MacKinnons, Armstrongs, Davidsons and Sinclairs. That should be fun. A gentle cultural shock for both Carvell Perley and Goordut Singh. But this year he wanted his Butler's Crossing Christmas to be without distractions; and a Butler's Crossing Christmas it was to be: tomorrow they would dine not on turkey but on chicken and roast pork, as their neighbours did.

His next stop was a shopping plaza, a staggeringly ugly purple and orange monstrosity flanked by a supermarket, Colonel Sanders Kentucky Fried Chicken, the Tower of Pizza, and a self-service filling station. The place reminded him of an essay he had read as an undergraduate in which H. L. Mencken argued that there was a libido for the ugly, a sensual wallowing in the hideous. Clayton supposed that it was the spiritual equivalent of vandalism.

From a battery of loudspeakers, there blared a recording of the Korean Orphans' Chorus singing, "The Little Drummer Boy." Everything in Woolworth's was made of plastic: there was plastic glass, plastic steel, plastic wood, even a fireplace made of plastic bricks and filled with plastic logs that gave off plastic flames. Still, it was apparent from the faces of the shoppers that here in this little city of 100,000 people, the corruption was not yet complete. Few here wore tight-lipped, flesh-coloured masks and had electro-magnetic eyes. Some of them actually smiled or nodded or said things like, "Some

crowd, eh?" in response to his murmured, "Pardon me,"
when he bumped against them.

He bought Barry a Junior TV Magician set. Barbara
would disapprove. "You knew very well it would be
nothing but a few scraps of cardboard and some bits of
coloured plastic," she would say to Barry; and then to
Clayton, "I thought we'd agreed that there'd be no
store-bought presents," using the words "store-bought"
to show that she wasn't really upset although of course
she was. And he would say, "This way he'll see for himself
what kind of rip-off artists he'll have to deal with for the
next fifty or sixty years." Then, probably, they'd laugh,
and he and Barry would sit down on the floor with the set
between them and he would study the directions.

In the parking lot, on his way back to his car, Clayton
met Bruce MacKinnon, who owned the farm next to his.
"Doin' some last-minute shoppin' are you, Professor?"
the old man said. Like many farmers when they came to
town, he was dressed more like an athlete on his way to a
game; his sporty slacks, jacket and cap, all of which
looked as if they were being worn for the first time, were
in marked contrast to his wind-burnt and mottled face,
his yellowish-gray hair.

"It's a madhouse in there," Clayton said.

"Just so long as they ain't sold out of Christmas cheer,"
the old man said. "Thought I might slip in and buy myself
a little bottle of it." He winked. "What the wife don't
know won't hurt her, I always say."

"I hope we'll see you tonight," Clayton said.

"Oh, you won't see me tonight, Professor." The old
man poked Clayton in the ribs as if this were the punch
line of a joke that he considered hilarious.

"I'm sorry to hear that," Clayton said, wondering what
it was that the old man found so funny.

"You won't be seein' nobody from Butler's Crossing."

"What makes you think that?"

"I don't think it, Professor. I know it. There won't be

one single solitary soul from Butler's Crossing at your place tonight."

Oh! It was part of the game. "But some other people might be visiting us, I take it?"

"Well, now, I wouldn't be surprised if you was right." The old man held out his hand. "Merrie Christmas to you, Professor."

"And a very merrie Christmas to you, Mr. MacKinnon."

"It's the magic of the mask," said Bob Warren, adjusting his sandwich so that the smoked meat would be less likely to slip out from between the two slices of rye bread when he raised it to his mouth. "The wearer becomes the person, animal or thing that the mask represents."

"A living folk ritual going on within twenty miles of this university. My God! Isn't it fabulous?" Clayton sipped from his glass of Dutch beer.

"You'll be disappointed, you know," Warren said. "It's pretty crude stuff. You and Barbara are expecting them to entertain you with a miracle play or some such thing. Actually it's more like Hallowe'en."

"It will be fun, anyway," Clayton said.

"They pretend not to recognize each other, of course, and that gives them a freedom they don't have at any other time. If you're not going to eat that pickle, could I have it?"

Clayton speared the pickle and transferred it to Warren's plate. "It should be interesting to see Butler's Crossing with its inhibitions down."

"It's a relatively harmless way of releasing the tensions that build up in a small, insular society. The university should devise something similar; we're another small, insular society reeking with suppressed malice."

Barry went to bed early, hoping in this way to trick the morning into coming sooner, after which Clayton went out to the woodshed and came back with the bobsled he'd had Gerrish Davidson make for the boy. "Three generations have slid down Eriskay Ridge on some of my sleds,"

Gerrish had said, spitting tobacco juice on the snow, and Clayton didn't doubt it. The sled was built to last, as was everything that the men and women of Butler's Crossing shaped with their hands. "This should last me out," they would say matter-of-factly of a quilt, a table or a chair that they had made, meaning that it would outlast their bodies, "and the young ones should be able to get some use out of it after I'm through with it."

"I hope he likes it," Clayton said.

"He'll love it," Barbara said. "Why wouldn't he?"

"It may turn out that he'd rather have one of those Flying Saucer things. I've seen a lot of kids around Butler's Crossing on them, and kids his age are awfully damn imitative."

"Not Barry."

"You sound like a Jewish mother."

"All mothers are Jewish mothers."

"I'd better start making the punch."

The beverage was known to the Scots as Het Pint and to Butler's Crossing as Moose Milk. He warmed and thickened beer, added sugar and spices, and spiked it with Teacher's Highland Cream. "My God," Barbara said, "the smell of it alone is enough to make anyone drunk."

"I had to pry the recipe out of Graham Munroe. You'd have thought I was asking him to betray a tribal secret." He took a cautious sip. "Hey, it's not bad. Surprisingly pleasant, as a matter of fact. Here. Try it."

"Later. I don't want to plunge head-first into the clam chowder."

"The chowder smells terrific." His lips brushed her cheek. "I think I'll put on a record. Something Christmasy."

He took down a recording of carols by Joan Baez. Adjusting the stereo set, he decided that his New Year's resolution would be to resume his guitar lessons. There were men and women here who could teach him the songs their grandparents had taught them. He also decided that during the holidays he would talk with Barbara about having another child. The world might be over-populated, but his world wasn't. He pictured himself celebrating Christmas thirty years from now in this same house, surrounded by his grandchildren. He grinned; that is what came of drinking Graham Munroe's Moose Milk.

Someone knocked loudly. "Here we go," Clayton said.

Eight or ten people stood on the steps or in the walk. "Will ye let the Mummers in?" The speaker wore a black hood; as he spoke the words, he inhaled deeply. "Come in," Clayton said, remembering too late that, according to tradition, he ought to have refused them admittance at first. Hooting, stamping their feet, scattering snow everywhere, some of them beating saucepans with wooden spoons, the Mummers entered.

They smelled of mothballs and of dusty attics and airless closets. Several of the men — now that they were inside, in the light, Clayton saw that they were all men —wore women's hats and dresses. One of them elbowed him so violently that he almost fell. The elbower, who wore a Red Devil Hallowe'en mask, laughed; and the others pounded their saucepans.

Barbara ladled hot punch into Irish porcelain mugs. "Do you know who I am, Professor?" demanded a man who wore a woman's stocking over his head and what looked like a nurse's cape over his shoulders.

"I'm afraid I don't," Clayton answered.

"He's afraid he don't!" Black Hood snorted.

"I thought you guys was supposed to know everything that there is to know," Stocking Head said. Clayton laughed. "Are you laughin' at me?" Stocking Head snarled.

"I'm laughing at myself," Clayton said.

"The Professor is laughin' at himself!" Stocking Head told the others. There was more beating of saucepans.

They were all of them very drunk, Clayton realized. He

raised his mug and, unable to think of anything to else to
say, said, "Merrie Christmas!"

Nobody responded.

"You haven't told us who you are," Barbara said to
Stocking Head.

"He's St. George," said the Red Devil. "He's St. George
and I'm Beelzebub."

Bob Warren might be right about their not remembering the old Mummers' plays, but at least they had not
forgotten two of the stock characters.

"I rescue fair ladies in distress," said Stocking Head.
"Tell me, fair lady, are you in distress?"

"I hope not," Barbara said.

"She hopes not," said the others, inhaling on the first
word and exhaling on the last two. Red Devil was not the
only one to wear a Hallowe'en mask; there was also
Dracula, Frankenstein's monster and what Clayton
guessed to be the Phantom of the Opera. Yet they didn't
look in the least silly, these muscular drunken men.

"Drink up, Professor," said Beelzebub, whom Clayton
had by now identified as Graham Munroe. Clayton drank.
If he kept this up, he would turn into a sleepwalker.

"Stop that, damn it!" Barbara said. There was a roar of
lewd laughter. Shaking the fog out of his eyes Clayton saw
that Stocking Head's hands were under her sweater.

"Hey, come on now," Clayton said to Stocking Head,
who called himself St. George and who spoke with Gary
Armstrong's voice. The dumb kid! he thought. Yet the
others weren't laughing good-naturedly at the boy; they
were laughing derisively at Barbara. He could single out
the shrill cackle of old Bruce McKinnon.

"You like to tease, don't you, fair lady?" Gary Armstrong said. "Runnin' around with no bra. Just beggin' for
it."

"The joke has gone far enough, Gary," Clayton said.

"I bet she don't wear no pants either!" cackled old
MacKinnon from the sanctuary of his Black Hood.

"Do you wear panties, Barbara?" said Graham Munroe, safe in the armour of Beelzebub.

"Come on, guys," Clayton said, "Let's all have another drink."

"Listen to the great Professor!" said Beelzebub. "The great Professor that has been doin' his damndest to keep us from gettin' our pulp mill."

So that accounted for their rancour. "It's Christmas, Graham," Clayton said.

"He thinks we don't know it's Christmas!" Beelzebub said. There was a great pounding of saucepans. In a remote corner of his consciousness, Clayton registered the fact that Dracula had thrown a burning cigarette butt on the floor and was crushing it out with his heel.

"There will be some pretty lean Christmases on Eriskay Ridge if him and his committee get their way," somebody said.

"It's not my committee," Clayton said.

"Him and his committee!" old MacKinnon said. "They don't like the smell of sulphur. They'll smell plenty of it in Hell."

More laughter, more pounding of saucepans. Somebody staggered against the table; there was the sound of breaking glass.

"I want you people to get out of my house," Barbara said.

"Darling," Clayton said.

"Clayton, I want these people out of my house. What kind of a Christmas is this?" She began to cry. "Damn!" she said. He knew how she despised herself when she cried. "Damn!" she said again.

Suddenly, the Mummers were silent; and, just as suddenly, Clayton was angry. Afterwards he was to reflect uncomfortably that he might not have been so vehement if their silence had not freed him from his fear of them. For he had been afraid.

"God damn it," he said. There was a shuffling of

heavily booted feet. 'We thought you people were our friends." Nobody spoke. "We thought we had found a home here." Oh, dear God, he thought, keep me from crying too.

"You don't understand, Professor," Graham Munroe said. He had taken off his mask.

"For Christ's sake, stop calling me 'Professor'!"

"Clayton, you don't understand. We're the Mummers. We act the fool this way in every house in the settlement."

"Like hell," Clayton said.

"I swear to God. A little farther down the road, we'll be giving somebody the devil for being *in favour* of the pulp mill. Oh, maybe young Gary went a little farther with your Missus than he would of gone with Bruce MacKinnon's old woman." There was uncertain laughter. "But he didn't mean any harm. He thought she'd get a laugh out of it. And, as far as the stuff we said to you goes — my God, man, that was mild compared to some of the things we've said to other people."

"We didn't treat you folks one damn bit different than we'd treat anybody else," old MacKinnon said. "Except we wasn't as hard on you. And that's the God's truth."

"The boys wouldn't of stopped here if it hadn't been for me," Carvell Perley said. His tone was apologetic. "We don't usually bother strangers."

They left quietly with murmured goodnights, still drunk but no longer the Mummers. Clayton helped Barbara clean up the cigarette butts and broken glass.

# A JUKEBOX
# IN THE KITCHEN

*"DID YOU HEAR* about Monique and the Gooks?" Stellarton said. She was peeling an orange with her fingernails. One of those angular woman whose angularity is as provocative as another woman's curves. Bare-legged, in a pale blue dressing gown. This was in Lizzie Richmond's place on Salamanca Street, before the call girls, the deer hunters' wives and Urban Renewal put brothels out of business. We often went there to drink at two or three o'clock in the morning, after the paper had gone to press. Donaldson, the night news editor, said that Lizzie ran a bootleg joint under pretense of keeping a whorehouse.

"That Monique!" Casey said. "If brains were gun-powder, she wouldn't have enough to blow her nose." She pulled her chewing gum out of her mouth and stretched it like an elastic band with one end in her fingers, the other between her teeth.

"Look who's talking," Stellarton said, dropping her orange peelings in a coffee tin that served as an ash-tray. Casey stuck out her tongue. Her gum fell out of her mouth.

"Make sure you pick that up," Pop said. He tended the door, in which there was a peep-hole with a shutter and marks that we pointed out to newcomers as bullet-holes. Perhaps they really were bullet-holes.

"What do you think I am?" Casey said.

"A cow," Stellarton said.

"Get off my back, Stellarton. For crying out loud."

At other times — on warm afternoons when they sat in the windows and laughed at, or with, the passers-by — they were like school girls when one of them brushes another's hair and the consciousness of the one drowsily mingles with that of the other.

"What happened to Monique?" I said. She was the youngest of Lizzie's girls, and a beautiful object if you avoided her eyes, which were badly crossed. On quiet nights, she sometimes sat on my lap and played the jukebox, reaching back from time to time for another coin. The amazing thing about the jukebox was that it was in the kitchen.

"She's in jail," Casey said

"Let me tell it," Stellarton said.

"What else is there to tell?" Casey said.

"I thought Lizzie had an understanding with the cops," Donaldson said.

"Sure," Pop said. "But this happened uptown."

"In a bank," Casey said. "I told you she was one dumb broad."

After my first visit, I had said to Donaldson, "A

jukebox in the kitchen!" And he had replied, "Where would you have put it, then?"

"Come off it," he was saying now. "You're putting me on."

"They didn't get her for hustling," Casey said. "She was —"

"Shut up," Stellarton said. "You'll spoil it. Let me tell it."

"Excuse me for living," Casey said. She unwrapped another stick of Spearmint.

It was a very old Wurlitzer, with a hole like a lake and a long, twisting crack like a river in the window in front of the turntable — set up in one of those huge Victorian kitchens that contained a sofa as well as a cook-stove.

"What did the Gooks have to do with it?" Donaldson asked.

The slots that were supposed to contain little cards giving the titles of the songs were empty. Not that this mattered; the records were never changed. Monique's favourite was Fats Domino's "Blueberry Hill."

"She ran into this guy uptown," Stellarton explained. "He was from one of those old tubs that have Wop officers and Gook sailors. The Wops were boozing it up at the Duke of Wellington Hotel. So the Gooks decided to have some fun themselves."

Next to "Blueberry Hill," Monique's favourite record was Perry Como's "Catch a Falling Star." Listening to the music, she was aware of me only to the extent that she would have been aware of any object on which she was seated.

"They didn't have any money," Casey said.

"They never have any money," Stellarton said. "That's what makes them Gooks."

Monique! She liked movies about real life, she said, especially when they starred Rock Hudson and Doris Day. Monique in panties and pullover. Beautiful enough, apart from her eyes, to inhabit a boy's dreams or reawaken an old man's secret regrets. Her hair tickling my cheek, my chin at rest upon her shoulder.

"Poor sad cow," Casey said. "She spent the whole damn night with a shipload of Gooks."

"You mean they forced her to go aboard?" I said. Donaldson laughed.

"Forced her, hell," Stellarton said. "They paid her."

"I don't get it. You said they didn't have any money."

"They had Gook money, dummy."

"Piasters," Pop said.

"No, no," Stellarton said. "They call them dollars, the same as we do."

"Hong Kong dollars," Donaldson said.

"Hong Kong dollars, King Kong dollars, what's the hell's the difference?" Stellarton said. "It's all play money."

I might have gone to bed with Monique if it hadn't been for Charlie who, as often as not, sat on the woodbox across the room. He wouldn't have objected. In fact, he would have been pleased, so long as she took my money and provided she wasn't wearing his ring. When she was working, she took the ring off her finger and gave it to him and he hung it from a white ribbon around his neck.

"A white ribbon!" I had exclaimed to Donaldson; and he had replied, "So buy him a black one."

I didn't go to bed with Monique because, even after a third double rum and Coke, I knew that I'd have felt dirty afterwards. Not because she was a whore but because all the time that Fats Domino or Perry Como or Ricky Nelson ("There'll Never, Ever Be Anyone Else But You") was singing, she stared at Charlie, a little man with a face the colour of an egg-nog — and her poor, deformed eyes were luminous with love.

"She stayed with the Gooks all night," Stellarton continued. "And the next morning, they paid her with their King Kong dollars. Thousands and thousands and thousands of them. Stuffed into her blouse and into her pants, even into her shoes and stockings. She thought she was the richest goddamn whore in the world."

Donaldson's blurted laughter sprayed the air with rum. I wondered where Charlie was.

"Wait," Stellarton said. "You haven't heard the best part. She kicked up a hell of a fuss in the bank. Accused them of trying to cheat her when they told her Gook dollars weren't worth the paper they were printed on. Started yelling, 'I'm rich! I'm a millionaire!' She was still yelling it when the fuzz dragged her away." Stellarton began to peel another orange, biting off and spitting out a bit of the rind. "Some sad, eh?"

# PRISONER OF WAR

*THEY'RE NOT EVEN* human. I know what I'm talking about. They're worse than niggers. I ought to know; I lived eighteen months with the bastards. You ask any of our fellows who were there. They'll tell you the same thing: they're lice.

It's the God's truth if I never rise from this chair. The Russians are the scum of the earth. Say what you like. They're pigs. You know what they used to do? I'll tell you what they used to do —.

The Jerries got the Bren Gun Carrier I was in. Wham! I didn't even know we'd been hit until I came to and the three guys that were with me was dead and everything

81

was on fire. That's how quick it all happened. Just "Wham!" and the next minute I was trying to get out and for a while I didn't think I was going to make it. Jesus. Jesus. The blood was streaming down my face and I thought sure as hell I was going to be roasted alive. But I got out somehow and staggered down the road, staggering from one side of the road to the other side of the road like I was drunk as a fool, the blood running down into my eyes so I couldn't see —.

I don't know how far it was I walked before I came to this farmhouse and went up to the door and knocked and this old French woman came to the door and took me in and tied a rag around my head and helped me to get into bed. I remember there was real starchy white sheets on the bed, real starchy but cool. It's funny, a man remembering that after all these years. About the sheets, I mean.

And then this Jerry officer was shaking me awake. There were two or three Jerries in the room and my head hurt — it hurt like hell. They sent me to Germany in a cattle car, me and a whole bunch of our fellows and Yanks and Limeys. And that's where I found out the kind of pigs the Russians are.

The POW camp we were taken to was split up into two sections. One was for the Canadians, the Limeys and the Yanks, and the other section was for the Russians. If the truth was known, I think the Jerries hated the Russians worse than they hated the Jews.

I didn't mind the Jerries. Most of the time they didn't bother us if we didn't bother them. I even learned a little Deutsch. But the Russians! Wait till I tell you about them.

Soup was what we ate, mostly. Potato soup, I guess you'd call it. Potato soup and black bread. Everybody said that the bread was made out of sawdust and it probably was. The meat in the soup was horsemeat, sure as hell. We were hungry all the time. I was hungry every minute of every day for eighteen months. Used to daydream about food. You get hungry enough, it's like wanting a woman. The same feeling, only a hell of a lot worse. If you were handed a steak, you'd rape it. Jesus!

The difference between us and the Russians was that we was civilized.

You know what those damn Russians used to do?

They used to eat garbage!

Every man of us would of starved to death before he'd of done that. I don't need to tell you what *that* garbage was like. Makes a man sick to think about it.

We used to watch them sneaking over to the garbage barrels, a few of them at a time, in those smocks and balloon-legged pants they wear, some of them in their bare feet because the Jerries liked those big boots of theirs. We'd stand there with our bellies stuck to our back bones and watch them stuff their faces. My God, to look at them you'd of thought they were eating lobster. They sure stuffed their guts. It was sickening.

Jerries used to drive them the hell out of there if they caught them, and they weren't gentle about it either. If they got close enough they'd wallop the greedy bastards with the butts of their rifles. But the minute the Jerries were out of sight, you'd see those bloody Communists slinking back for another big feed.

One of our fellows had of tried that, the rest of us would of knocked the living bejesus out of him.

Once in a while there would be some of us who couldn't stand watching them any longer, and we'd put the run to them. And you know what? The bastards thought we were driving them away so we could have that stinking garbage for ourselves!

Having the lousy pigs think that was even harder to take than watching them eat.

# THE YEAR
# OF THE REVOLUTION

*THE YEAR IS* 1969. The Year of the Revolution. At King George University in New Maryland, Canada, the Robber Baron treads on the supine bodies of the People or, to be precise, is lifted over them, they being sprawled on the steps of the Central Administrative Building, commonly known as Old Victoria Hall.

"A pretty kettle of fish," the Robber Baron says to the President of the University who, in the same manner as the Robber Baron, has been passed from one pair of Commissionaires to another, over the heads, knees and elbows of the young men and women singing, "We shall not, we shall not be moved," each of the Commissionaires thinking the same thought, "Please, God, don't let me have a heart attack," and wishing fervently that he had drunk less beer and eaten fewer Royal Canadian Legion pickled eggs in the quarter-century since Sicily or Normandy. A photograph will appear in the student newspaper, which is now controlled by Trotskyists, they having ousted the Maoists the previous week. It will show the Robber Baron aloft; "fleeing from the just and righteous wrath of an aroused People," the caption will say.

"A pretty kettle of fish," the President of the University will say when he sees it, not only there but on the front page of the *Daily Intelligencer*, where it will illustrate a story headed *Reds Harass Philanthropist*. "A petty cradle of itch. A pedant crushed in a ditch." He will then swallow three capsules of Librium and in a little while fall asleep at his desk, only to dream that the Robber Baron stands before him in his rimless eyeglasses and Prussian colonel's haircut, and signs cheque after cheque, payable to the University, tears cheque after cheque into shreds, until the carpet is littered with confetti that might have been an astronomical observatory, a school for veterinary medicine —. Why in God's name hadn't he stuck with the Department of External Affairs? It were better to be torn limb from limb by a mob of wogs in Khartoum.

His private secretary awakens him.

"What is it, Ayesha?" Ayesha is his secret name for her. She Who is Older than Time and Must be Obeyed.

"I beg your pardon, sir?"

"I'm sorry. I'm afraid I was . . . preoccupied. What is it?"

"More bad news, I'm afraid, sir."

He learns that a coalition of Trotskyists and Anarchists has occupied the office of the Vice President (Academic) on the grounds that he is a neo-Fascist, racist pig, he having refused to implement a guarantee that at least fifty-one per cent of the faculty would be black, Hispanic, oriental, Amerindian, Métis or Eskimo. ("Indian" and "Eskimo" have not yet been denounced as vulgarisms, and the daughters of the bourgeoisie have yet to discover that they are among the oppressed). The Red Flag of Socialism and the Black Flag of Anarchy hang from a third-storey window of this very building, Ayesha says, and from that same window there emerges strange music: the recorded voices of the men of the 15th International Brigade singing songs of the Spanish Civil War.

'A perry kettle of fish indeed," the President sighs. "A putrid cartel of kitsch in seed." In the student newspaper, until recently known as *The Georgian* and now calling itself *F.U.*, the office of the Vice President (Academic) is designated Free Zone No. 1, as in an editorial beginning, "Our sisters and brothers remain steadfast on the barricades of Free Zone No. 1., despite an ineffectual attempt by the dupes and lackeys of neo-Fascist, racist Imperialism, masquerading as students of forestry, to stem the inexorable tides of World Revolution by immorally confiscating a quantity of the People's Food Supplies," in the form of three six-packs of Coca-Cola and ten orders of Colonel Sanders' Kentucky Fried Chicken. "They shall not prevail," the editorial goes on to say. "We shall not be moved. Soon the oppressed workers and peasants will rally to our Cause. They will come from every corner of the province, marching with fists upraised in salute, and together we shall overthrow the Running Dog University administration and the Comprador pseudo-government which sustains it. Arise ye prisoners of starvation!"

To which, the *Daily Intelligencer* replies, "Regular readers of these columns do not need to be reminded that the *Daily Intelligencer* has not infrequently added its voice to those raised in advocacy of a return to the birch as the most efficacious form of rehabilitation for those young hooligans euphemistically described today as

Juvenile Delinquents. Juvenile Delinquents? Balderdash. dash. Commenting on the decline of corporal punishment in the schools of his day, the Great Cham of 18th century English literature, Dr. Samuel Johnson, said that what the scholars had gained at one end, they had lost at the other. Observing the imbecile shenanigans now rampant on the campus of our provincial University — an institution supported by the hard-earned dollars of the average taxpayer and the generosity of that beneficent individual denigrated by these miscreants as 'Robber Baron' — all right-minded, clear-headed, and clear-thinking people must feel a twinge of nostalgia for the disciplinary rod."

During this period of his life, the President of the University, as befits the son of an Anglican Bishop, will often recall how King David incurred the Divine wrath when he sought to number the Children of Israel. For the President had incurred the wrath of the People in a similar way. He had approved the introduction of identity cards for both faculty and students.

From a practical standpoint, the identity cards were unnecessary, since this was a small university in a very small city. But identity cards stood for Progress; and New Maryland, of which the President was a native son, no more questioned Progress than it questioned Tradition. In fact, the President, who had felt equally at home at both Oxford and Columbia and who subscribed to both *Punch* and the *New Yorker,* neither of which he had ever been known to describe as boring, often referred to Progress and Tradition as the twin pillars — the Boaz and Joachim — of the contemporary Temple of Solomon.

To Professor Sandoval, whose kindlier critics explained that he had been hit over the head by a Chicago policeman's riot stick during the 1968 Democratic presidential convention, the identity cards had a different and darker significance. "The Nazis started out in exactly the same way," he reminded anyone who would listen. "They issued identity cards to the Jews. Are you aware that plans are being made to put every inch of this campus under surveillance by closed circuit television cameras? Yes, Comrades, the Robber Baron and his cohorts are watching us, and the concentration camps are ready and waiting in Alberta."

The existence of the concentration camps was confirmed by Professor Rosscoe, a member of the British Israel World Federation and the Monarchist League, who said it was only a matter of time before there was a general clean-up of Zionists, Freemasons, Bolsheviks, dope fiends and other unwashed, longhaired, bearded weirdos, including Professor Sandoval who was, besides, an American and therefore a member of a mongrel and mutinous race. Professor Sandoval, for his part, predicted that one day soon, Professor Rosscoe would be hung from a lamp-post.

Professor Rosscoe's disgust at Professor Sandoval's having said "hung" when he ought to have said "hanged" was militated by his pleasure in the prediction. "He says they're going to hang me," he reported happily to his wife.

"Dear me," she said, and went on preparing dinner.

"Is that all you have to say?" Professor Rosscoe said. "The man says he is going to hang me."

"Oh, I'm sure the President would never allow that," she said. "After all, Professor Sandoval doesn't even have tenure."

Professor Rosscoe preferred to believe that his help-meet was upholding the great Anglo-Saxon tradition of using dry humour to alleviate fear. He patted her arm. "There's no use playing the ostrich, my dear," he said. "I must be prepared, if necessary, to go to the scaffold for my sovereign and my God, as many good men have done before me."

"Dinner is ready, dear," she said. Professor Rosscoe sighed deeply.

While Professor and Mrs. Rosscoe dined by candle-light on Frankfurters wrapped in bacon and Kraft cheese slices, elsewhere in the city Professor Sandoval and his companion, Katrina, were sitting down by candlelight to brown rice and bean curd. "Rosscoe says I'll be one of the first to be locked up," Professor Sandoval was saying happily.

"Of course you will, my darling," said Katrina, who before the Revolution had called herself Suzanne. "I have only to close my eyes to see you being led away in chains like the student Raskolnikov." Her parents had named her Barbara.

"Katrina, Katrina," Professor Sandoval said. "How many times must I warn you against that kind of petit bourgeois sentimentality?"

"I'm sorry," she said.

"Don't be sorry," he said. "Be self-critical, in the spirit of the Great Helmsman. Before you can eradicate the bourgeois elements from society, you must learn to eradicate the bourgeois elements in yourself."

"Eat your dinner, dear," Katrina said.

"Stop sounding like a wife," said Professor Sandoval.

"I am your wife," Katrina said wickedly.

"For God's sake, Katrina," said Professor Sandoval. They had legally married just before legal marriage became unfashionable. "You know as well as I do that we'd be of no use to the movement if that ever came out."

When the identity cards were introduced, Professor Sandoval had gone to the university library, having first filled the pockets of his jeans and carpenter's smock with toothpaste, dental floss, mouthwash, shampoo and two kinds of deodorant, spray and roll-on, in case he had to spend the night in jail. His arms laden with books gathered at random, he had proceeded to the check-out desk.

"That's a lovely evening, Professor," said the woman at the check-out desk, opening a book — it was *Science and Health with Key to the Scriptures* — and slipping a card into a slot.

"Haven't you forgotten something?" Professor Sandoval said.

"I beg your pardon?" she said.

"You didn't ask me for my identity card."

"Oh, I know who you are," she said.

"That's not the point," Professor Sandoval said to the woman, who was now processing a copy of the authorized biography of Prince Rainier of Monaco. "The new regulations make it mandatory that you examine my identity card before allowing me to take out books."

"That's a lot of nonsense, if you ask me. Well, here are your books, all ready to go. My goodness, do you think you can carry them all? Let me get a bag for you."

"So that's the game, is it?" the Professor said. "A strategic withdrawal, doubtless by order of the President. Well, it's not going to work. I demand that you ask for my ID card."

"Well, if you insist . . ."

"I emphatically insist."

"All right then, show me your identity card."

"I refuse to do so," said the Professor.

"That's okay with me," she said.

"It is not okay with you," the Professor said. "You must now refuse to permit me to remove these books from the library."

"Oh, I couldn't do that," she said. "You're a member of the faculty."

"You can, you must and you will," said the Professor.

"No, no," she said. "I couldn't possibly do that. You'd have to talk to the chief librarian."

"I must warn you," said the Professor, "if you do not refuse to permit me to remove these books from the library, you will be guilty of an infraction of university regulations which could result in your dismissal."

"Do you mean I'll be fired?"

"That is precisely what I mean."

"All right then, if you put it that way." She drew a deep breath. "You can't take those books with you."

"Not unless I show my identity card."

"Not unless you show your identity card."

"Then I will leave these books here — on the floor — as a gesture of non-violent resistance to your Fascist conduct," the Professor said. "Later today, and in the days and weeks ahead, many members of the Students', Workers' and Peasants' Coalition for Free Speech will do as I have done."

"Oh, dear," she said.

"I must also remind you of the precedent established by the Nuremberg trials of War Criminals," the Professor continued. "Don't think for one minute that you can escape the People's vengeance by pleading that you were only following the orders of the Robber Baron and his hired prize-fighters, such as the Running Dog President of this university. By the way, what is your name?"

"Miss Winthrop," she answered meekly.

"Winthrop Must Go!" read many of the signs that were carried by the students who picketed the library the following day. Others read, "Heil Winthrop!" "Winthrop, Warmonger," "Winthrop, Fascist Stooge," and "Winthrop Up Against the Wall!" There were speeches in the parking lot by Professor Sandoval, and by Itchy Gaucho Bingham, president and, as a matter of fact, only member of the campus branch of the Young Communist League, who was soon after to defect to the Trotskyists and thereby cause a leading Trotskyist monthly, published in New York, to carry a front page story announcing that at a university in Canada, the young Stalinists had been converted *en masse* to Trotskyism, which was cited as further proof that World Revolution was imminent.

Following the speeches, the demonstrators burnt effigies of Miss Winthrop, the President of the University, the Robber Baron, Lyndon Johnson, Hubert Humphrey and Adolf Hitler. "The panty raid they used to have made a lot more sense to me," an elderly Commissionaire was heard to mutter before an increasingly menacing chant of, "Off the pigs!" caused him to withdraw to the boiler room, where he had stashed a mickey of gin. The Commissionaire's remark was thought worthy in the next issue of the student newspaper. "The Cossack gentry howled obscenities at the People," the paper said.

Commenting editorially on the demonstration, the *Daily Intelligencer* calls for an end to permissiveness in the home and a ban on blue jeans in the classroom. In a letter to the editor, Professor Rosscoe urges that certain of his colleagues be charged with contributing to the delinquency of the minors under their care and supervision. Another letter writer points out that nothing of this kind happened during Prohibition and suggests that today's students merely pretend to take drugs in an attempt to conceal the fact that they are addicted to alcohol.

"A pretty kettle of fish," says the Robber Baron. "A plethoric cauldron of twitch," says the President of the University, who can hear the stereo player in Free Zone No. 1 playing, "All we are saying is, give peace a chance."

"Be firm," Ayesha counsels him. "Remember Louis XVI. If he had shown an ounce of firmness, there would be a Bourbon on the throne of France today." The President's private secretary has often said that the world has been going to hell in a handbasket ever since 1789, and nowadays one can't even find a decent handbasket.

"I could give them Miss Winthrop easily enough," the President muses. "She could be transferred from the library to the groundskeeping department and re-educated through manual labour and closely supervised self-criticism. I might even give them the Vice President."

"It's the Commissionaires you ought to get rid of," Ayesha says. "Pot bellies and bifocals. They ought to have been replaced years ago, preferably by a bunch of tough young townies, the kind who think that all college boys are poufs."

"One thing is certain," the President says. "I can't back down on the identity cards. A university without identity cards in this day and age would be like a town without shopping plazas. If we do away with identity cards, none of our professors will ever again be asked to deliver a paper to the Learned Societies of Canada."

"And the Canada Council would be sure to reduce our grants," Ayesha reminds him. "The Canadian Association of Universities might even take away our accreditation."

"Yes," says the President, "and the Robber Baron would refuse to accept another honorary degree. That would mean there would be no astronomical observatory, no school of veterinary medicine." He puts his head in his hands.

"For want of an identity card, the university was lost," Ayesha says.

"Exactly!" says the President. They sit silent for a moment, listening to the recorded voices of Harry Belafonte and Miriam Makeba singing a Zulu war song.

"A guerrilla must live among the People as a fish lives in the sea," Professor Sandoval is telling the occupants of Free Zone No. 1.

"Right on!" says Itchy Gaucho Bingham.

"Like, wow, man," says Tick McSamuels, the Revolutionary Poet.

"We've got to take our message to the masses," says Professor Sandoval. "To the wage slaves of the Robber Baron and his ilk."

"Up against the wall," says Itchy Gaucho Bingham.

"Like cool, man," says the Revolutionary Poet.

"That means we've got to liberate the park," says Professor Sandoval. "As they did in Berkeley."

"Far out," says the Revolutionary Poet.

"All power to the People!" cries Itchy Gaucho Bingham. Other voices take up the cry. "All power to the People!" Hearing it, the President of the University swallows four Librium capsules. Soon he is again asleep at his desk, dreaming that a fiendishly laughing Robber Baron in a white hard hat is using a wrecking ball to demolish the gymnasium which he donated the year that he was made an honorary Doctor of Humane Letters.

That night an Ad Hoc Collective of Students, Workers and Peasants was organized to liberate the city park, with Professor Sandoval as chairman. The Professor's first act in that capacity was to telephone the Chief of Police. "I must warn you that we have no intention of applying for a permit to march," he told him. "And I must also warn you that we intend to violate the park curfew."

"Like in Berkeley, eh?" said the Chief of Police.

"Like in Berkeley," the Professor agreed.

"Then I must warn you that I intend to enforce the law," said the Chief of Police. "This is it," he said to the Mayor and City Solicitor a few minutes later. "Here's our chance to stomp on those Commie bastards."

"Bloody right," said the Mayor. "I didn't fight and die in World War II so that a bunch of bloody Reds could hand this country over to a bunch of bloody Chinamen."

"We'll hit them with everything we've got," said the Chief of Police.

"There are a couple of problems," the City Solicitor said.

"What kind of problems?" the Mayor demanded.

"They don't need a permit to march," the City Solicitor told him unhappily.

"Why not?" the Mayor wanted to know.

"There's no by-law on the subject," the City Solicitor explained, sounding even more unhappy than before. "You know as well as I do, nobody ever marches in this town except the Canadian Legion and the IODE."

"Then we'll nail them for violating the park curfew," the Chief of Police said.

"I'm afraid that's another problem," said the City Solicitor. "There's no curfew on the park. Never has been."

"Good God!" said the Mayor. "We can't let the people in Montreal and Toronto find out that we don't even have enough on the bloody ball to put a bloody curfew on the bloody park. We've got to do something. Call an emergency meeting of City Council."

"No good," said the City Solicitor. "You have to give three weeks' notice before adopting a new city by-law."

"We can't afford to wait that long," said the Chief of Police. "Sandoval and his Commies will be in the park tonight."

"And there's not a bloody thing we can do," the Mayor said. "We'll be the laughing-stock of the country."

"There's one possible way out," said the City Solicitor.

"Speak up, man, what is it?" said the Mayor.

"We could ask Sandoval to postpone his march," the City Solicitor said.

"Why in God's name would he agree to that?" asked the Chief of Police.

"He can't very well protest if there's nothing to protest against, can he?"

"It's worth a try," said the Mayor. He picked up the telephone. "Get me Professor Sandoval at the university," he told the switchboard operator.

The negotiations between the Mayor and Professor Sandoval took up the better part of an hour. At one point, the Professor suggested that the problem be solved by his publicly burning the Canadian flag; the City Solicitor regretfully informed the Mayor that it was not against the law to burn a Canadian flag. It was finally agreed that it would be in everyone's best interests if the occupation of the park was postponed. Among other things, this would give the Police Department time to equip itself with non-lethal means of riot control, such as rubber bullets and mace.

The following day it was announced on mimeographed notices on every bulletin board on the campus that a Mass Teach-in of Students, Workers and Peasants would be held in the park in three weeks' time. In that same day's issue of the *Daily Intelligencer,* the Mayor gave notice that he would introduce two new by-laws, one requiring any organization wishing to march in the city to obtain a permit from the Chief of Police, the other establishing a 10 p.m. curfew on the city park.

So, while Professor Rosscoe was not hanged, Professor Sandoval did indeed go to jail, if only for a night, as did several other member of the Ad Hoc Collective of Students, Workers and Peasants. "They'll hang me yet," Professor Rosscoe promised his wife. "Of course they will, dear," she said, and patted his arm.

But, in fact, death came to Professor Rosscoe not at the end of a rope, but at the end of a dinner, in consequence of heart failure brought on, it is believed, by the excitement of hearing ex-Czar Simeon II of Bulgaria address the annual congress of the World Monarchist League at the Savoy Hotel in London.

Professor Sandoval had by then abandoned both politics and teaching. After leaving the university, he and Katrina-Suzanne-Barbara had at first gone into sheep-farming, on the theory that they could thereby provide themselves with all of the necessities of life, making their meals from lamb or mutton, supplemented by wild fruits and berries, clothing themselves in homespun and lighting their log cabin with tallow candles, thus escaping from what Professor Sandoval now referred to as, "this dreadful century."

When next heard of, they were in San Francisco, where Katrina-Suzanne-Barbara was among the editors of a feminist magazine called *Slut,* and the Professor was producing documentaries for the Public Broadcasting

Service, and taking an active part in the Gay Liberation Movement. Most recently, Dr. and Mrs. Sandoval — Katrina-Suzanne-Barbara now calls herself Ruth — have become widely known as Born Again Christians, appearing regularly on the same television talk shows as Charles Colson and Elridge Cleaver. Rumour has it that, like Bob Dylan, they were baptized in Pat Boone's swimming pool.

Miss Winthrop had, of course, been fired for her mishandling of the identity card crisis at the university library. The President of the University had been appointed Canadian High Commissioner to Tonga and Fiji. The Robber Baron had been swallowed up and absorbed by a multinational corporation, in much the same way as a snake swallows and absorbs a toad. Itchy Gaucho Bingham was rising rapidly in his family's fast food franchise operation. Tick McSamuel, the Revolutionary Poet, was teaching computer science and running a real estate business on the side. The elderly Commissionaires had been replaced by young men with moustaches who spent their spare time working on their motorcycles and practising the martial arts. Only the *Daily Intelligencer* and Ayesha, She Who is Older than Time and Must be Obeyed, went on as before. Because by now it was 1970 — and 1975 — and 1980 — and the rhythm of life kept changing, as if there were seasons in a century as there are seasons in a year.

Thunder sounds a lot like laughter when the storm is far enough away.

# *INFIDELITY*

*BELONGING AS HE* did to that dimin-
ishing section of society that still believes in marriage,
Tim Bohan at thirty-five was not simply an unmarried
man; he was a bachelor. It was assumed by his friends that
he had not merely declined to make one kind of commit-
ment, but had elected to make another.

On Saturday nights, he was usually to be found in the
Marco Polo Room of the Admiral Beatty Hotel, watching
the NHL game on television. For one season, when he
was nineteen, he had been paid to play hockey for an
ostensibly amateur team in northern New Brunswick. He
wasn't quite tough enough or quite fast enough, even for

that league, but as he said: if there was any salt in his beer it had come out of a shaker and was not from his tears. Since then he had knocked around the country a bit, working for newspapers in North Bay, Ontario, and Brandon, Manitoba. Now he was back home in Saint John, employed by the provincial government as an information officer. He often said that the only good thing about his job was that it was a hell of a lot better than having to work for a living.

Tom looked younger or older than his years, depending upon one's reaction to his unfashionably short hair. "It's not a statement of principle; long hair makes my ears itch," he explained. His friends were men married long enough that their wives and children had ceased to cling or need to be clung to. He golfed, curled and played poker with them and ran into them at horse races. They seldom invited him to their homes — reasoning, he supposed, that no man in his right senses would willingly go where custom ensured that half of those present would be middle-aged housewives.

He had no women friends. That is to say that he had no friends who happened to be women. In his circle there was no provision for such a relationship; a woman was your wife, your mother, your daughter, your sister, your girlfriend or your whore. He might address a friend's wife as Isabelle, but they were never really Tim and Isabelle to each other: they were Friend's Wife and Husband's Friend. As such, they would not have dreamed of, say, having lunch together, just the two of them, except perhaps if they had accidentally met in a restaurant at lunch-time, and then they would both of them have felt very uncomfortable and even slightly wicked.

Women were scarcely less mysterious to him now than they were when he had cringed in the confessional as a pubescent boy and been tormented by the lipstick stains — ah, how blasphemously lascivious those lipstick stains had seemed to him! — where painted ladies had kissed the crucifix.

He had lain with many of them over the years since he had lost his innocence in the back seat of an eight-year-old 1952 Pontiac. That had been a series of mild electric shocks, preceded by idiocy and followed by embarassment. He had not told the priest about it, although he never neglected to confess the sins of the imagination; perhaps this was because the reality had seemed less sinful than ludicrous. The thirty-five-year-old Tim usually laughed during intercourse and often tickled his partner so that she laughed with him. When asked why he had never married, he said it was because he liked women too much; the questioner could take this whichever way he pleased.

Nowadays the girls didn't switch their tails when they saw him approach as they once had done. The field was narrower; many of the entries had been scratched and the track had become a trifle muddy. He had more or less given up the young stuff. It was too much work: smoking pot when it only gave him the same drowsy, uneasy feeling that booze had given him at the beginning, twenty years before; keeping in mind that they had rejected the old verbal tabus based on sex and adopted new ones based on race; having to let his hair grow until it itched like a bastard. Anyhow, as often as not they had frizzy legs and bramble in their armpits.

When he felt the need for a female body he generally rented one. "It's like hiring a plumber," he told his friends. "I don't take the plumber out to dinner. We don't dance with each other. When my drain pipe is clogged, I pick up the telephone, send for someone who can do the job, get it done as efficiently as possible and pay for it in cash."

Susan Morrison first caught Tim's eye by skating well, skating exquisitely in comparison with anyone else on the ice that afternoon. Until he ran out of breath, he was better than most skaters of half his age, if he did say so himself, but he was not in the same league with this lady. She might not belong on an Olympic team, but she was as close to it as anyone you were ever likely to find in a Saint John arena during a free skating period. "You're so good it's embarrassing to be on the ice with you," he told her.

She was dark-skinned and dark-haired, dressed in a white turtleneck and a tartan skirt. He guessed her to be eighteen; later he was to learn that she was twenty-five. They had coffee and doughnuts in a little diner near the arena. He learned that she had come from a little place in Nova Scotia where "there was nothing to do in the winter but skate" and was a nursing assistant at the Catholic hospital. She declined his offer to drive her home.

The following weekend he ran into her again and they skated together. She laughed at his jokes, and there is nothing that makes a woman look so beautiful to a man as that. Over coffee, they found that each was a creative audience for the other, which is how most human relationships begin. "Susan," he said, after bringing his Dodge Dart to a stop in front of her apartment building which, like many of the cheaper Saint John apartment buildings, was actually a Victorian mansion which had been converted into flats. "Susan, we can't go on meeting like this. What do you say we have dinner together some night this week?"

"All right," she said. He realized, suddenly, that her answer had been very important to him.

"Will you have something from the bar before dinner, Mr. Bohan?" Tim hoped she had noticed that the waiter knew his name, and then inwardly laughed at himself for being so boyish.

"Live dangerously," he said to her. "Have a Pink Lady."

"Okay," she said. "A Pink Lady."

"That's the spirit. And I'll have a rye and ginger ale. A double." He picked up the menu. "Now, what are you going to have to eat?"

"I hate menus," she said. "I can never make up my mind what I want."

"Take your time; there's no hurry."

"Poached salmon?" She sounded like a schoolgirl replying to a teacher's question and not sure if her answer was correct.

"Tell you what," he said. "Let's have the *steak au poivre*. They flame it in cognac."

"Okay," she said. And, later, when the waiter flamed the steak at their table, "I've never seen them do that before, except on television."

Tim laughed and raised his glass of California wine. "To our noble selves," he said. "That's a toast they give in Ireland." They clinked glasses and drank.

"Have you ever been in Ireland?" she said.

"Sure," he replied, untruthfully.

"I've never been farther from home than St. John's, Newfoundland."

"What were you doing in Newfie John?"

"You won't believe this."

"Try me."

"I was in a convent."

"You were a nun? You're kidding."

"Not a nun, just a novice."

"I won't ask why you left."

"I just didn't have a vocation, I guess."

"So now you're a nurse."

"A nursing assistant. It's not much of a job, really."

"Have some more wine," he said, reaching for the bottle. It had been a long time since he had met a woman like this one, the kind you had to know how to undress. He would distract her with little nibbling kisses on her neck and ear-lobes while he undid the top button on her blouse, and from there he would procede cautiously to the clasp on her brassiere (he was grateful to observe that she wore one), at the same time kissing her on the mouth so that she was free to pretend not to know what mischief his hands were up to. His voice would be very gentle, his hands would be very firm, the one assuring her that he would assume the entire responsibility for what was about to happen, the other letting her know that they had passed the point where she had any real say in the matter.

"Good night," she said. They were standing in a hallway where a century earlier a house parlourmaid in a lace cap would have disdainfully directed a mick like him to the tradesmen's entrance at the rear. Now it contained a panel of mail slots and buzzers and was lit by a 40-watt bulb in a pseudo-antique wall fixture. The place smelled of lemon oil and Kraft Dinner.

She had turned her head so that the kiss intended for her lips had merely brushed her cheek. Tim grinned; this was so much like the old days. The only difference between the few women he had dated in recent years and the many he had hired was that the former cost a little more and took up a little more time. Ordinarily, it was one or two Pink Ladys, dinner at the Beatty and then a session of slap and tickle at his or her apartment. This one was different. "You're beautiful," he said, his mouth close to her ear. She pushed away his hands — not roughly, but with finality. "Good night," she said again.

On his way home, he picked up a program of "Golden Oldies" on the car radio. Frank Sinatra was singing "Nancy with the Smiling Face." The song suited Tim's mood perfectly.

He didn't telephone Susan the next day. Instead he called Denise, whose first words after they got out of bed were, "I could use a cold beer."

She padded about his apartment with an open bottle in one hand and a hunk of Polish sausage in the other, using her teeth to tear the cellophane off the sausage. She was naked except for a pullover sweater.

Afterwards, he stood for an unusually long time in the

shower, scrubbing himself, then cleaned his teeth and gargled with Listerine.

"Have dinner with me tonight." This was three days later; it never paid to appear over-eager. Like the old newspaperman that he was, he held the telephone between his cheek and shoulder, leaving his hands free.

"I can't; I'm sorry."

"Tomorrow night then."

"I'm afraid I'll be tied up tomorrow night too."

"I get the message," he said, and immediately afterwards cursed himself for sounding like a pimply adolescent.

"No, it's not like that at all. Listen, would you like to go to a play with me Saturday night?"

"I'm afraid I'll be tied up Saturday night," is what he ought to have said. Instead, he heard himself say, "What time will I pick you up?"

The play was *The Diary of Anne Frank*. At the end of the first act, she borrowed his handkerchief. "It's a good thing I don't use eye make-up," she said. "Nobody ever considers the fact that the mess his family got into was old Frank's own fault," he would have said to anyone else. "They had money; they could have gone to England if he hadn't been so damn worried about his bloody factory." With her he smiled, almost paternally, and said nothing.

Although Tim loathed country music — as a native of a small city in a predominantly rural province, he was defensively contemptuous of hicks — he and Susan drove to Fredericton the following week to hear Johnny Cash. Susan jingled like a teeny-bopper when she found that Prince Charles, in New Brunswick on manouvres with his regiment, was unexpectedly in the audience, a very slight, unshaven young man in a blue blazer and desert boots, his face both remote and quizzical. "He's cute," Susan declared.

"Yeah," Tim said. "He ought to make some thirteen-year-old girl very happy." They were in the parking lot, after the show. She ran ahead, stopped, made a snowball and threw it at him. "For that, I'm going to rub your nose in the snow," he warned her.

"You'll have to catch me first."

He chased her, caught her chiefly because she had been laughing while he'd saved his breath, then rubbed snow in her face until both of them were gasping. Like all children's games, this was at bottom intensely serious. She was in his power — "in his power" described it exactly — her legs clenched between his, her wrists locked in his fingers. Alternately, he forced her to lie perfectly still and allowed her to squirm, in this way defeating her not once but again and again, until at last, having learned that it was futile to struggle, she lay motionless even when he relaxed his grip.

"You're not fair," she said, sounding pleased with him.

"What's going on here, buddy?" It was a policeman, with a pistol strapped to his rectangular body. Tim and Susan picked themselves up. "You okay, lady?"

"Perfectly okay, Constable," Susan said. "We're making bloody fools of ourselves, that's all."

From that night on, in all sorts of situations, she said to him, "What's going on here, buddy?" or he said to her, "You okay, lady?" Out of every kind of human intimacy, there emerge the rudiments of a new language.

Tim was seen much less often in the Marco Polo Lounge. He and Susan skated and swam together. He would rent a room at the hotel so that they could use its indoor pool. In her presence, he was only vaguely and disinterestedly aware that the room contained a bed.

"I was taught to swim in the old-fashioned way," he told her once. "We went for a picnic in the country, the whole family, Dad and Mom and the five of us kids. There was a lake and Dad just grabbed me and threw me in. Sneakers, jeans and all." He laughed. "I learned to dog-paddle pretty damn fast, I can tell you."

"That was cruel," Susan said.

"Cruel?" He had almost forgotten how he had screamed. "Maybe it was."

"I'm not sure that I'd like your father."

"The old man's okay. When I was a kid, he was away from home all week — he was a travelling salesman all his life. Every Friday night when he came off the road he'd have some kind of pet for us. A pup or a kitten. Once it was a rabbit. No matter what it was, Mom gave it away as soon as Dad left."

"Why?"

"Why what? Oh. Mom's allergic to cats and dogs. Or claims to be. The old man says there's no such thing as an allergy. Claims it's all in her imagination. They're quite a pair. One of these days I'll take you to meet them."

"I'd like that," she said.

They watched the New York Rangers play an exhibition game in Moncton. "I love magicians," Susan said, so they went to see the Amazing Armstrong and Tim almost forgot that he found sleight-of-hand artists boring. At a wrestling match, they cheered the villain until the hero's fans began to pelt them with bottle caps. They even went to church together once, to a folk Mass at which, to Tim's discomfiture, a red-bearded young man in a caftan played a guitar and sang lyrics that seemed to consist of the word "yeah", endlessly repeated.

Each time he drove her home, walked her to her door, kissed her good night and went, unprotestingly, on his way.

It was as if he were a boy again and the female population were divided, as it had been in his boyhood, into working class girls who would do it and middle class girls who wouldn't.

The more he saw of Susan, the more strongly he suspected that she was a virgin. It was by no means impossible; she had been in a convent, an uncle was a priest. Besides, Tim believed that decent women had no deep desire for sex; it was a common saying among his friends that a man married the worst screw he had ever had. Far from being frustrated, he derived a satisfaction amounting almost to exhilaration from leaving Susan's chastity intact.

Once or twice a week, he summoned Denise; if she wasn't available, he telephoned Yvonne.

"What's your sign?" Susan asked him, They were crossing the harbour bridge in his car.

"My sign?"

"Your astrological sign, dummy. When's your birthday?"

"Oh. September. Libra."

"That's good. I'm Aquarius. We're supposed to be very compatible."

Alone in his apartment, Tim poured himself a stiff shot of Gordon's gin, put an Al Hirt album on his stereo set and lay down on the chesterfield to do some serious thinking. Then, he realized that he wasn't trying to reach a decision, but rather celebrating a decision he had already made. What the hell, he would ask Susan to marry him.

They had dinner at her place. She had cooked spaghetti in a sauce robust with pepper and garlic; he had brought Chianti. Having eaten at a card table by the light of a single homemade candle, they sat on the rug in front of the fireplace and drank Drambuie.

"I like you a lot," he told her.

"Me too," she said.

He took her hand and squeezed it, her fingers echoed his. "I love you," he said. Had he ever said that to anyone before? He kissed her neck, her hair tickling his lips. Their mouths met and, to his astonishment, he felt her tongue worm itself between his teeth. He drew back. "I shouldn't have done that," he said.

"You didn't do anything; I did." Her face turned away from him, towards the fire. "What's the matter with me, Tim?" The question startled him.

"I don't know what you mean," he said.

"It's obvious that you don't want to make love to me."

"My God, the first time we were together you practically slapped my face!"

"You were too damn sure of yourself that night." She laughed and inched closer. "Make love to me now, Tim."

He kissed her. She pulled up her skirt, past the tops of her stockings. "See, no pantyhose; they turn you older guys off, don't they?"

He laid his hand on the inside of her thigh; she began to unbutton his shirt.

"No!" He pushed her hands away.

"For Christ's sake," she said. Then, "Are you gay, or what?"

"You bitch," he said.

"I think you'd better leave."

"Come here."

"You'd better leave."

"Shut up," He grabbed her by the shoulders and spun her around. "Take down your pants and get down on your knees."

"I don't like Neanderthal men, Tim. If that's what turns you on — " He forced her to her knees. "God damn you," she said. He pulled up her skirt, lowered her panties, parted her knees and entered her from behind. She ceased to resist him except with her will and, after a few moments, her will gave way too.

"You liked it, didn't you?" he said to her.

"Not like that," she said. "My God."

"Don't lie; you loved it."

"My God, you didn't even take off your pants."

He laughed harshly. "You'd better pull yours up," he said. "It's hard to express righteous indignation when your ass is bare."

When he left Susan's apartment that night, Tim was almost certain he would never marry. Yet he believed he knew how a husband felt upon learning that a wife whom he loved had been unfaithful.

# TRUE CONFESSION

*SHE COULD REMEMBER* how pleased
Arleigh had been when she told him, soon after they'd
started going together, that he reminded her of a western
gunfighter, she wasn't sure which one, maybe George
Montgomery, certainly somebody younger than John
Wayne and tougher than Audie Murphy; he'd walked
with that easy slouch, his arms not swinging much, hands
never moving far from his hips, stooping a little, his eyes
half shut, and he'd drawled, wrinkling his nose, making
his voice sound more casual and throaty than usual when
he got angry.

All the boys wanted that look. But none of them could

do it so well as Arleigh. Barbara thought of this now as he came into the kitchen and threw the black lunch pail on the chair nearest the door.

He walked straighter now. Over the past two years she had watched the tension increase in him, his body stiffen, his shoulders grow hard. She had seen him coming to look more like his father, like her father, like all the men at the sawmill, and the transformation baffled and frightened her.

He sat down and swung his chair around, away from the table. Bending forward, he unlaced his gum rubbers, then kicked them under the chair and stood up in his wool socks.

Barbara rubbed her palms on her jeans, shook salmon from a can on to a plate.

"Hot, ain't it?" she said shyly.

Every day she grew more shy with him.

"Yeah, I guess so," he said.

He undid the two top buttons of his plaid shirt and pulled it over his head. At the sink he washed himself in cold water, his eyes closed, grunting.

"I guess every summer gets a little hotter than the one before, somehow," she said.

"Yeah." He rubbed his face briskly with a towel. Yellow flecks of sawdust were shaken out of his hair. Despite the scrubbing, bits of sawdust were still entangled in his two days' growth of beard.

He put on his shirt and sat down at the table. She filled his plate with boiled potatoes, canned peas and salmon, hurrying because he did not like to be kept waiting for his food, and poured strong black tea into his cup. Then she sat down opposite him. He bent low over his plate, his right hand wielding his fork, his eyes focused on nothing, his mouth to be kept full from now until he finished.

"You have enough stuff in your lunch pail today?" she asked him.

"Yeah. Sure. I guess so. Why?"

His voice was muffled and distorted, his cheeks puffed out with food.

"Oh, no reason especially. Just wonderin', that's all."

"Oh."

He bent back to his plate, forgetting her again.

They completed their supper in silence. She wished he would talk to her, although she knew there was nothing to say. He was not irritable, she knew. His silence was masculine and matter-of-fact. It was a silence that she had watched expand and envelop him since he had married and gone to work in the mill.

It means he is a man, no longer a boy, she thought. But she could not accept it quite, not yet. The memory of his loud, insolent laughter was too fresh. She felt something curiously similar to jealousy, as though the mill, the men with whom he worked, the whole ritual of manhood as they knew it, had somehow seduced him and robbed her. But she pushed such thoughts away, because all deep thoughts disturbed her. She was not equipped to control them: they distracted and confused her, and she was mortally afraid of being pretentious or over-imaginative, what she believed to be "odd" or "foolish."

He finished eating, cleaned his plate out with bread, and crossed the floor in his socks, loosening the belt of his denim pants and patting his belly. While she washed the dishes and cleaned the oil cloth table cover, brushing crumbs on to the floor to be swept up later, he lay on the couch smoking a cigarette, staring sightlessly at the smoke as it curled up toward the ceiling.

"How was everythin' at the mill today?" she prodded him, resenting the complacency with which he withdrew from her.

"Same as it allus is, I guess," he said, not sullenly quite, but as though the question were meaningless and unnecessary.

Not George Montgomery, she thought. Maybe it was Myron Healy. He's the fellow who always gets killed.

He's gotten killed whenever I've seen him in the movies. Every single time.

"Arleigh," she said suddenly.

"Yeah?"

"Mebbe we could go to the movies in town this Saturday night. I hear they're showin' a real good movie."

"Mebbe."

"You mean we'n go?" Her voice became tense with eagerness.

"I dunno, Barb. Movies are kinda kid stuff, ain't they? I mean, a man works all week, he wants to kinda see the boys. You know — have a few beers."

"Yeah." Her excitement died.

"Mebbe we'n go. We'll see what happens between now and then. Okay?"

"Yeah."

Her work done, she took a magazine from the shelf which held the radio and sat down at the table again. The first story was entitled *I Couldn't Help Loving Him.* Opposite the title there was a photograph of a man and a girl locked in each other's arms, his mouth crushing hers. They were standing under a streetlight in the city and the man wore a suit, the girl a beautiful white dress, its neck cut low, his coat over her shoulders.

She glanced at Arleigh. Already he had fallen asleep. She began to read. Idly at first, her mind on other things. From time to time, Arleigh stirred. Once, without waking, he groaned and flung out an arm. Absorbed in the story now, she did not look up but only smiled tenderly.

# THE QUESTION

*"THERE MUST BE* other men in my position who are troubled by the same question," Kenneth McLellan told himself. "It's not something they'd talk about, even if they were drunk. But there must be times when, for one reason or another, they start to think about it, as I did this morning — yesterday morning," he corrected himself, because it was now 3:30 a.m. and another day. He was seated at the kitchen table in a dressing-gown and pajamas. Having been awakened as usual by the necessity of emptying his fifty-year-old bladder, he had let the cat out and was now waiting for her to pat the window with her paw to indicate that she wished to be let back in.

This morning — yesterday morning — he had done what he did every day except perhaps for a day or two in the winter when there was a genuine blizzard. He had got up, put on a gym suit, splashed cold water on his face, combed his hair (which was gray but as thick as it had ever been) and gone out for a two-mile run. He was in far better shape than most men of his age. He had to be. He was a soldier. A fifty-year-old soldier — a real soldier, an infantryman like Kenneth McLellan — had to keep himself in close to the same physical condition as when he was fifteen years younger.

It could be done, but as he had often remarked to his wife Leslie, it required fifteen times as much effort. This was only the first of three runs he would make before the day was out, in addition to the push-ups, the weight-lifting, the swim, and if there was time, the squash or tennis.

"I learned a lot when I was in India," he sometimes said to people. "Especially from the Jains. They teach that every day of his life, a man ought to do something for his body, his mind, and his soul." For his mind, he played chess or read history. For his soul, he listened to music — he liked Chopin — or gave the price of a bottle of wine to a panhandler.

"They don't deserve it," Leslie would say.

"That's why I give it to them," he would explain.

On this particular morning, she was waiting to show him something in the newspaper that had been delivered during his absence. "If it's another damn silly announcement from the minister of national defence, I don't want to see it until after breakfast," he said, on his way to the downstairs bathroom to take a shower. But he stopped and took the paper from her, looked where her finger pointed.

There had been an attempted military coup in a West African country where he had served as a military attaché. "I'm surprised it hasn't happened before this," he said. "Heavy fighting in the capital city . . . Sources express fear that this could be the beginning of a full-scale civil war . . . Has there ever been a half-scale civil war? . . . The commander of the insurgent forces is —"

"Jimmy."

"Jimmy," McLellan echoed. He sat down with the paper in front of him, but what he saw was a very black, very slender, very humorous young man. "Jimmy. It's hard to picture him leading a revolutionary army."

"It's hard to picture any of them doing the things they've done."

"It is indeed."

Before being given his present command, McLellan had spent several years as second in command of an infantry officers' training program. Each class had included cadets from various countries in Africa and Asia. The McLellans had often entertained these young men in their home. It was expected of them, of course, but they had enjoyed doing it as well. They had felt especially close to those who, like Jimmy, had come from countries where McLellan had served as an attaché.

"This one is apt to be messy," he said.

"Yes."

"The old boy would probably be content to retire and go into exile with a whole skin, but I can't see his tribe giving up their perqs without putting up one hell of a fight."

"I'll turn on the radio."

"Okay." McLellan had rather liked the old boy. They had exchanged stories, the old boy telling him about his experiences as a Sergeant with the King's African Rifles during the Second World War, McLellan talking about Korea.

But it was the cadets that he thought about as he showered. They had eaten lunches and dinners at the McLellans', played games or listened to recorded music.

Some of them had learned to skate on the miniature ice rink that had been created behind the garage by the McLellans' sons. They had taken many photographs to send home to their families. Then they had gone home themselves and, shortly afterwards, put the training that he had helped to give them to use.

He continued to think about them as he ate the breakfast Leslie had prepared for him, tomato juice laced with powdered Vitamin C, a single slice of unbuttered whole wheat toast, a low-fat omelette made from egg-whites and yellow food-colouring. There was Joshua, who had led a battalion during a civil war in Chad; Mohammed, who had become a national hero in Bangladesh; and, "What was that young Libyan's name, do you remember, the one who was mad about backgammon and got wounded in Uganda?"

"I know the one you mean, but his name has slipped my mind too. There were so many of them."

"Um." His atttention turned to the radio. "There it is."

"I'll turn it up."

There had been conflicting reports, the radio said. McLellan smiled grimly at the pun. Only one thing was certain, it appeared. Heavy fighting continued.

"Well, I'd best be on my way," he said. "This morning I'm going to take a surprise look at how the boys on the Green Line are doing." His lips pecked her cheek, her lips pecked his. "I'll have lunch at the mess."

"Fine and dandy."

A little later, he climbed into a jeep and was driven out to the Green Line by an aide. "They're doing a pretty realistic job of it out there," the aide said.

"Greeks" and "Turks," played by soldiers, most of them NCOs, who had done at least one tour of duty on Cyprus, were making life as complicated as they could for the youngsters with rifles and bayonets who manned the line that was supposedly meant to separate them. One "Greek" had managed to acquire a donkey, which he had allowed to wander on to "Turkish" territory. A "Turk" had collapsed, ostensibly from old age and exhaustion, on the "Greek" side of the road. Competing loudspeakers played Greek and Turkish music. The two sides threw stones at each other.

"They're not kidding either," the officer in charge told McLellan with obvious satisfaction. "At least, not completely. The longer they keep at it, the madder they get."

"How are the kids taking it?" McLellan asked.

"Some of them have got a bit rattled; but that's the purpose of the exercise, isn't it? I think we'll have them whipped into shape by the time they're faced with the real thing."

"Of course the real thing won't be real either. At least we hope it won't."

"Pardon, sir? Oh, yes, I see what you mean."

A red-faced young private was striving to persuade the "Turks" to return the "Greek" donkey. One "Turk" kept pushing him away so violently that each time he was almost knocked off his feet. The others hooted and howled at him. Another young private, this one white-faced, tried to bring the "Turk" who had collapsed to his feet and at the same time to shield him from the "Greeks," who heckled him and pelted him with handfuls of dirt and pebbles.

"Carry on then, Major," McLellan said.

"Right you are, sir."

"Let's go back to the office," McLellan told his aide.

"Sir?"

"I said, let's go back to the office."

"Very good, sir."

Ordinarily, he would have enjoyed the play-acting on the Green Line. He had enlisted because the army would pay his way through university, which he couldn't have afforded as one of four children of a village grocer. He had stayed on because he liked the theatrical aspects of military life, the dress uniforms, the ceremonial swords, the trooping of the colours, the mess dinners on the anniversaries of the battles whose names were inscribed on the regimental flag, the absurd and splendid traditions — most of which had been crammed into green plastic garbage bags and dispatched to the dump by those damn politicians.

Today, he saw only the absurdity, none of the splendour. Perhaps he was getting old.

There was no damn "perhaps" about it.

He *was* getting old. This would be his last Command before retirement.

The younger officers were under the impression that he had fought in Korea. They had heard him tell stories about the fighting there, which he in turn had heard during his early years with the forces from officers only slightly older than he was. He had never consciously intended to give this impression. On the other hand, he'd have made himself look ridiculous if he'd gone around telling them that they were mistaken and that in fact the war was over by the time he received his commission.

He had served creditably in West Germany, and with the United Nations forces in the Sinai and on Cyprus. He had been in command of a regiment during the October Crisis in Quebec; and whatever people said about it now, this had seemed important at the time. Hadn't both the hands and the voice of a minister of the Crown been shaking when he, the minister, asked if he, McLellan, was absolutely certain that the loyalty of the French-speaking officers could be depended upon?

He and Leslie had been comfortably married for almost as long as he had been a soldier. They had reared three children, none of whom had caused them to suffer public shame or prolonged vicarious pain. When he retired, he and she would spend their winters in Bermuda. She painted in watercolours. He would devote more time to his chess and his military history. They both liked to swim; and perhaps they'd buy a little boat: a sloop or maybe even a schooner.

Most of the time, he was content. And that, he

reflected, was as much as anyone had a right to expect at fifty. But today the question troubled him, as it had done occasionally during the war in Vietnam, when Americans of his generation were leading troops into combat. Now, waiting in the kitchen for the cat to pat the window with her paw and be let in, he phrased the question this way:

"I am Brigadier-General Kenneth McLellan, Member of the Order of Military Merit. Holder of the Queen's Silver Jubilee Medal. I have been a soldier for a quarter of a century. In all that time my country has never gone to war. So I have never been called upon to kill a human being, and no human being has ever tried to kill me. I have never once heard a shot fired in anger; and now I will die without knowing how I would have felt and what I would have done."

# MOTHER AND SON

*OCCUPATIONAL THERAPY,* it's called.
There are about a dozen of us who trundle carts similar to
those you have seen on railway station platforms from
the huge, underground kitchen with its steaming pots,
mounds of peeled vegetables, and hairy-chested cooks in
open shirts and tall white hats, down a long, white crypt-
like tunnel to the dumbwaiters that carry baskets of
boiled eggs, vats of Irish stew and, on Sundays, hot roast
beef wrapped in tinfoil, up to the wards. Twice a week, on
Mondays and Wednesdays, we go from ward to ward,
supervised by an attendant with a jangling key-ring, each
team of two men carrying a hamper, made from canvas

sewn on to a steel frame, stuffed with bundles of filthy clothing and bedding tied up in sheets.

We leave our own wards at eight o'clock in the morning and go back to them at five o'clock in the afternoon. Since we do not work more than three or four hours a day, we spend more than half of the time sitting around in the tunnel or, rather, in one of the many storerooms, most of them empty, joining it. We are all of us on ground parole, which means we can come and go much as we like provided we do not leave the grounds, so the attendants do not watch us as they do the inmates from the back wards who sandpaper furniture and rake leaves off the superintendent's lawn.

The storeroom where we usually spend much of the day is situated far down the tunnel and contains several hundred bedsprings in stacks five or six feet high, with spaces like passageways, about four feet wide, on all four sides of each stack.

We play cards — poker in all its forms from five card stud to hooks, crooks, one-eyed jacks, moustached kings, and a pair of natural sevens takes all; cribbage, casino, blackjack, Russian bank, rummy, bridge and even euchre. We analyze the previous night's game between the Boston Bruins and the Montreal Canadiens. We debate whether Joe Louis in his prime could have beaten Mohammed Ali in his. We discuss women or, more accurately, we discuss Woman. Czerny tells us how he once spent a weekend in Havana in bed with a jug of sherry and two beautiful nymphomaniacal Cuban sisters. Fullerton disgusts Dominic, who as always sits very close to Jimmy, whom he calls Giacomo, by saying that his own tastes are so catholic that the inaccessibility of women does not disturb him. "I don't think we should talk about that kind of stuff in front of the kid," Dominic says. Jimmy-Giacomo blushes as prettily as a pageboy in a novel by Baron Corvo, and Fullerton laughs.

And we have Belafonte, the West Indian, who is called Belafonte because sometimes he claims to be Belafonte, and sometimes he says that he is Belafonte's son or younger brother, and sometimes he says simply that Belafonte is the greatest singer in the world. Belafonte —our Belafonte — sings Belafonte songs, accompanying himself on the guitar. His favourite is "Island in the Sun."

When we're wanted, Mickey Levesque, the attendant in charge of our detail, goes into the furnace room near the mouth of the tunnel and pulls the cord of a steam-whistle three times. "Boots and Saddles," Fullerton calls it. Usually, we are quick to respond, for Mickey, retired foreman of a railway section gang, has no patience with loafers and while he cannot fire us he can put us on report, and a man who is put on report is almost invariably confined to his ward.

The only part of the job I heartily detest is collecting dirty laundry in the women's wards. The back wards in the men's section are horrible too, full of creatures that look, act and smell like Swift's Yahoos. But they do not upset me as much as even the best of the women's wards.

When I was in Ward M2, the insulin ward, the women undergoing insulin shock treatments were in a ward adjoining ours and there was a glass window in the door between us. The door was near the attendants' office, and so we could go near it only when the attendants' changed shifts and, for a few moments, left the office empty. Then some of the men would talk to the women through the glass. It was adolescent teasing, mostly, natural enough because none of us on Ward M2 was much older than twenty. But the women — girls, really — frightened me. I knew they had an equal right to be afraid of me. I was an inmate too. But their hysterical eyes and moist lips terri-fied me in almost the same way as the novels of Bram Stoker and H. P. Lovecraft had terrified me when I was younger. Looking though the glass at them, I could believe in hags and vampires and if that sounds ridiculous, well, as Czerny says: "What's the use of being crazy if you don't act like it?"

But let me tell you what happened recently. One morning about a month ago we were gathering up dirty laundry as usual when a woman on one of the back wards came rushing up to me, shouting: "Nicky! It's you, Nicky! I knew you'd come. Oh, Nicky! Nicky! Nicky!" Before I realized what she was up to, she had thrown her arms around me and kissed me on the cheek. The female nurses dragged her away, and there was a good deal of laughter at my expense. "She thinks you're her son," one of the other women explained. "Every once in a while she sees somebody she thinks is her Nicky. The last time it was an intern." The rest of the day, Czerny and Fullerton called me, "Nicky."

I thought that would be the end of it, but the next time we went through her ward, the woman spoke to me again.

This time she sidled up and addressed me in a whisper: "Nicky darling, I knew you'd come back. I knew you'd never forget me. You're all I have now that your father's gone. This is a terrible place, Nicky. You'll get me out of here, won't you?"

She must have been beautiful once and would have been handsome even now if it had not been for the wildness in her hair and eyes and clothes. As it was, she looked like a city in riot. Anarchy had broken out in her mind and spread throughout her body. "Don't leave me here, Nicky," she pleaded as I stood staring at her, hoping that the nurses would overhear and take her away.

"I'm not your son," I told her.

"Don't tease me, Nicky," she said.

"Listen, I'm not who you think I am. You don't know me. I'm a patient here the same as you are."

"You're being very silly, Nicky," she said. "But I love you anyway," and she kissed me again.

By now we were ready to leave. I pulled away from her and picked up one end of a hamper, while Fullerton lifted the other.

"Don't leave me, Nicky! Please don't leave me!"

I had to calm her. I was afraid that she would grab me again.

"It's all right; I'll be back," I said. "Don't worry."

"Say you love me, Nicky! Say you love me!"

"Yes, yes, I love you," I said, as we followed the attendant out the door. Didn't Fullerton laugh at that one! But what else could I do?

After that, there was no escaping her, and I found myself fostering her delusion; at first simply to calm her, and then, I suppose, from pity. I never actually told her that I was her son, but I no longer denied it. I am ashamed of that now. Perhaps, unconsciously, I encouraged her not because I pitied her but because it amused Fullerton and Czerny, and caused Dominic to tell me repeatedly that I was a most compassionate young man. What schizophrenic could resist appearing in a drama in which he played both Christ and Lucifer?

It was all very silly.

She was always near the door, waiting for me. Her appearance began to improve. She combed her hair, put on a little make-up, and wore a clean housecoat. Mrs. Lindsay, the attendants called her — so I must be Nicholas Lindsay. Well, I had not been notably successful playing the part of myself; as Nicholas Lindsay, I was unlikely to do worse.

"Good morning, Nicky darling," she would say.

"Good morning," I would reply. "You're looking very good this morning." It was true that she did.

"I feel much better, Nicky. The doctors tell me there's been a big improvement. But I don't need them to tell me that. I can feel it."

"Well, take care of yourself."

"Nicky?"

"Yes?"

"When are you going to take me home? I try not to be impatient, but I'd like to know."

"The doctors — they'll have to decide that. But you're looking better every day, you really are."

"Don't leave me here a day longer than you have to, Nicky, please."

"It's up to the doctors — "

"Please, Nicky —"

"I'll do my best."

Occasionally, the women from one of the churches in the city send us boxes, and the contents are often incredible: a jar of peanut butter, a package of pipe cleaners, a rosary, mittens, chewing gum, and a tin of anchovies may be found in one box, while another contains a copy of *The Imitation of Christ,* a wedge of cheese, a jar of cold cream, a penlight, a bottle of Pepsi Cola, and a Red Sox baseball cap. The last time these boxes were distributed, about two weeks ago, I actually found a rose in mine — a single, long-stemmed rose — which I could not resist giving to Nicholas Lindsay's mother.

I had become fond of her, you see. I suppose it flattered me to see how her face lit up when I entered the ward. It was like giving a coin to a beggar and buying a moment of sainthood for a quarter, although that is not how I thought about it at the time.

I was giving her happiness, and if it was based on a delusion, what the hell, was not all human happiness based on delusions of one kind or another?

In a little while, I might have started to call her, "Mother." It is even possible, God knows, that I might have come to enter into her dream and come to believe that I was her son; here we are constantly becoming participants in one another's delusions and hallucinations.

Last Wednesday, we collected the laundry as usual, and as usual, Mrs. Lindsay was waiting when we entered her ward.

"Good morning," I said cheerfully.

"Good morning, Nicky." She stared at me coldly. "That is your name, isn't it?"

"My name — " I began to edge away. What was she up to?

"You bastard," she said. "You dirty, little bastard!" Her voice rose, and an old woman walking by with a towel and a bar of soap in her hands stopped, looked at me with red, hate-filled eyes and laughed.

"Don't get upset," I pleaded. Fullerton was observing everything with a smile of pure delight. Czerny and the others were already in the bathroom, filling their hampers.

"Don't get upset, he says! The nerve of the son of a bitch! He lies to me, tries to convince me he's my son, and then he says, 'Don't get upset.' What kind of a fool do you take me for, you miserable little jerk?" She raved on and on, berating me. A crowd of women gathered around us, some of them simply curious, others urging her on.

"Look," I said helplessly. "Listen."

It took four attendants to subdue her. "You lying bastard!" she kept screaming. "You lying bastard!" I could hear the other women screaming it after me, even after we went outside and the attendant locked two heavy doors behind us.

# *WALKING*
# *ON THE CEILING*

*THERE ARE TIMES* when he feels
nothing except a passionate reluctance to die. Intellectu-
ally, it is possible for him to be stoical, even urbane,
about the certainty of his ultimate extinction. There are
even moments when his brain takes a savage satisfaction
in the knowledge that it will sooner or later cease to
exist. But the brain is not the man. There is a precogni-
tion of death that pervades the entire being so that what
you experience is not fear, in the ordinary sense, but a
terrible, vertiginous sense of wonder, such as you might
feel while floating helplessly in infinite space.

To Kevin O'Brien, this sensation is as difficult to

describe as its antithesis: the achingly mysterious realization, first experienced as a small child, that there is something so inexplicable as to be almost maddening in the simple fact of being alive. Many, many times over the years he has suddenly felt the strangeness of being himself, of being inside this body, of being conscious of the external world, felt this with the force of an unexpected stab of pain so that he would shut his eyes until the darkness turned purple, and shake his head violently, unable to formulate the question let alone arrive at an answer.

At the moment, Kevin O'Brien is not thinking about death, although he knows that he may be dead by this time tomorrow. He is not thinking about death, but the thought of death is there. Once, years ago, he bought a cheap alarm clock that ticked so loudly that at first he could not sleep in the same room with it. Its ticking was like the hammer from a child's toy carpentry set — he had been given such a set when he was a child — tapping, tapping, tapping on his forehead. He took the clock downstairs and left it in the living room but found when he got back to bed that he could still hear it. So he went downstairs again, and this time he put the clock in the porch, on a couch, and covered it with a blanket. Yet within a week he could lie within arm's reach of the clock without being aware that he heard it; and, later, when it stopped in the night, he would wake up almost immediately, knowing that something, he was not sure what, had gone wrong. Death resembled that clock.

He lies naked now, a sheet thrown across his loins, like a fallen soldier in a neoclassical painting, like Wolfe or Montcalm in "The Fall of Quebec." A nurse with long, slender fingers massages his back. At intervals, she pauses to pour more alcohol into her palm, afterwards rubbing her hands together briskly to warm them before applying them again to his flesh. He loves her, as he loves all the nurses, with a love that is infantile and incestuous. He does not wish to make love to them; he wishes they would make love to him, wishes they were free to caress him with their lips as well as their hands. They lull rather than arouse him. It is as if his body, in the face of death, had gone back to its infancy.

The little student nurses, doll-like in their starched white Alice-in-Wonderland caps and aprons, are all of them virgins. Kevin has said that to one of his visitors, who misunderstood him, of course, and laughed. But it is true. Their virginity does not depend upon their hymens being intact; in fact, it has nothing to do with the men they may have gone to bed with. (Kevin hopes that there have been many such men, each of them unknowingly a surrogate for him.) No, their virginity consists in this. Their innermost selves have yet to be penetrated by life. They are untouched — virgins who measure urine and plunge needles into fat, hairy buttocks. Their innocence is egocentric rather than sentimental; it can even be brutal. Occasionally, like everyone else, they imagine that they are playing at being something, when in fact it is what they are.

Among the older nurses there are a few who like men, love them even, only so long as the men are enfeebled or in pain. Such a one is Thurston who, having oiled him with alcohol now pats him with baby powder, pressing her breasts against his bare body; drowsily, voluptuosly, caressing herself rather than him. But, of course, this is not what they talk about. She talks about a film she saw last night, and he murmurs little wordless sounds of agreement.

Afterwards, Dennison, an orderly, shaves his chest and neck with a safety razor. He also shaves off the hair for three or four inches above his right ear. While this is being done, the ward supervisor brings a paper for him to sign in which he absolves the hospital from blame should the operation kill him. "It's like the preliminaries to an execution," Kevin says to her. She looks so annoyed that he adds, "I was only joking," and laughs.

He has visitors. The Susskinds, Maurice and Ruth, both of them on the faculty at the university. Before his illness, they were his friends and if he recovers they may be his friends again, but in the meantime they either bore or disgust him. Because of the Susskinds and others like them, he has decided that intellectuals ought not to be permitted to visit anyone who is sick enough to die. As Maurice and Ruth talk to him in horrible abstractions, the one quoting Heidegger and the other Bonhoeffer, Kevin waits for an orderly to come and shove an enema tube into his anus. The trouble with people like the Susskinds, he decides, is that they do not know there are times when it is wisest to stop thinking.

He does not tell them this. He has never told them how tiresome he finds them now. Not because it would be unkind to do so, but because it would be impolite. Trained in the manners of the middle classes, he would more than likely be polite to his executioner.

"Take off the pants of your pyjamas, please, and bend over. All the way. That's it." There is a legend that all hospital orderlies are homosexual. That is nonsense, of course. Still, the administration of an enema is a form of buggery. It would seem less degrading if the orderly inserted his penis. That would at least be human contact, flesh meeting flesh. The hard rubber tube is a defilement, an obscene instrument; and Kevin, grown paranoid, suspects that this may be intentional: the enema having been used as long ago as the Dark Ages to flush out demons. The semi-liquid excrement gurgles out of him, and he vomits. Tonight the Susskinds lent him a book by John Middleton Murry, *The Conquest of Death*.

He pits his will against the Nembutal, although he is fully aware that it is futile, even masochistic, to do so. It is intended to put him to sleep; and the paradox is that while he seldom refuses it, he is never able to restrain himself from fighting back when it begins to overpower him. He watches *Bonanza* on television. The actors look as if they were trying to conceal their utter, mindless self-satisfaction by feigning boredom. But then, Kevin remembers, the most popular television performers wear expressions of unprotesting boredom almost constantly. No matter what act they are engaged in on the screen, their faces look as if they too were watching television.

After a little while the Nembutal takes over and it becomes impossible for him to follow the plot. Nothing seems to bear any relationship to anything that came before it. The Nembutal pushes him deeper and deeper into the darkness, as if it were smothering him under the cotton wadding from a billion pill bottles.

He picks up *Nexus* by Henry Miller, one of the very few writers he finds it possible to read here, but his eyes refuse to focus. The radio is playing a medley from *The Desert Song* as he falls asleep.

The dreamer does not ask how or why he came from where he was to where he is. Kevin is in the basement of the Wingate house in his native village. It is a long, low farmhouse at the end of a lane, about one-half mile from the road. When they were children, Kevin and his sister Stephanie were left there occasionally overnight or for a weekend when their parents were away from home. Three very old people live in the house, two brothers and a sister whom almost everyone in the village calls Aunt Tetty. There is a parlour containing a carpet, the first Kevin has ever seen, fringed floor-length window curtains, an organ and a bookcase with a glass door. Everything in the parlour is brown: nutbrown, cinnamon, chocolate, mahogany. Children are forbidden to enter it.

The room in which Kevin and Stephanie are put to bed is a kind of garret, a right-angled triangle directly under the peaked roof. They lie on a mattress stuffed with feathers. This is how it used to be, and Kevin does not recall ever having been frightened there. But he is frightened now, terrified. Because the basement is a crypt, a mass of tunnels crammed with crumpling coffins, great stacks of them, and corpses in various stages of decomposition. He cannot find his way out, and it is very dark. He is frightened almost to the point of madness. And even as he dreams this, he knows that he has dreamt it many times before. It is not so much a dream, in the ordinary sense of the word, as an experience that he knows better than to remember, except when he is asleep.

Weeks ago, the night he was admitted to the hospital, he prowled through the building half the night, debating whether to throw himself from a window into the parking lot four storeys below or slip out of the hospital and drown himself in the harbour. The nature of his disease is such that one day it may become almost imperative that he kill himself. Moreover, he will have to do it in cold blood; that is, sentence himself and be his own executioner while he is still in love with life, because later there will be neither the ability nor the opportunity to accomplish it. The alternative will be to die obscenely, a living mind imprisoned in a corpse.

That night, roaming through the fluorescent corridors, he contemplated running away from the hospital, buying a bottle of gin and driving toward Quebec or the United States border — as though in Montreal or Boston he could elude death! The few nurses and technicians whom he encountered ignored him. Probably, since he was fully clothed, they took him for an employee. He found himself in rooms crowded with machinery: X-ray cameras, equipment for testing the heart, lungs, stomach, liver, kidneys, intestines and brain. He stumbled in and out of storerooms containing shelves of rubber tubing to fit every orifice of the body. Finally, in a broom closet, he broke down and wept. The tears purged him so that the following day he was joking with the other patients. By the end of the week, his reputation as a comedian was so well established that he felt obliged to be funny even while he suffered through the artificial sunstroke caused by the radioactive isotopes they had given him.

Not that it is hard to laugh. There is a young fellow in the ward, an olive-skinned French-Canadian farm boy with an anachronistic Robert Taylor moustache, who likes to play cribbage and talk about the Honda he is going to buy when he goes back to his job in the oil refinery. One day a visitor, having asked him how he was and being told there was something the matter with his blood, said very cheerily, "Oh, well, then if that's all that's wrong, you won't be here long." Every patient within hearing burst out laughing, and kept laughing until the tears came. Because they knew damn well that the visitor was right. The boy was not going to be here long. Not with leukemia. It seemed hilarious that this poor fool from the outside should say it in that kindergarten teacher tone of voice.

They joke about the hearses that arrive every morning at the rear entrance, which can be seen from the windows, to pick up the previous night's corpses; and once the young policeman whose bed is opposite Kevin O'Brien's played a trick on one of the student nurses: he pretended that he was dead.

Now it is morning. He has rehearsed this moment so often that now that it has come there is an unreality about it, as if time had stopped. A nurse who has called him by name a hundred times now examines his identification bracelet to make certain that he is the person he is supposed to be. Then she injects a sedative into his hip. The nurse and an orderly clothe him in a shirt that scarcely reaches to his navel and stockings that are like the legs of Baby Bunting pyjamas. They tie a funny little cap like a Victorian housemaid's cap on his head, and put bars along the sides of his bed. He senses that the purpose of all this, as of many of the rituals performed in hospitals, is magical rather than medical. Then again, it is as if he were being initiated into a sex cult as described in one of those English magazines such as *Victorian Erotica*. He wonders if he is about to discover something important about the relationship between sickness, sex and magic.

There are wheels on the bed. The nurse and the orderly push it down a corridor. They stop for a moment or two opposite the open door of an office in which a man, evidently an intern, is talking on the telephone with his wife. She wants him to stop at the supermarket on his way home and pick up a pound of ground beef, a bottle of soda water and a loaf of whole wheat bread. Kevin knows this because the intern repeats the name of each item into the mouthpiece and writes it down in a notebook. Kevin simultaneously envies and despises them for devoting time to such a trivial matter as groceries on the day that he may die. Surely, the whole world ought to pause to acknowledge that Kevin O'Brien is about to do battle with Death. He smiles, knowing that his death will be of no importance to anyone except himself and perhaps to the few people who love him. Sometimes this knowledge made things better; sometimes it makes things worse.

The wings of the operating table are like the arms of a cross. "It's like being a bit player on the *Dr. Kildare* show," Kevin says to the nebulous faces hovering above him. He prepared that remark yesterday, so that he would have a joke to show them that he was not afraid. None of them laugh. He is so exhilarated by fear that now he is intoxicated rather than numbed by it. He finds it amusing that they have tucked what he supposes to be his case history, a sheaf of papers attached to a clip-board, under the sheets by his foot. He has no idea why that should seem funny. The nurses are ugly in their hairnets and shapeless green smocks.

"This may sting a little," the anesthetist says. With one hand he grasps Kevin's wrist, with the other he slaps Kevin's forearm briskly and repeatedly. Then he sticks a needle which seems to be shaped like a fish-hook into a vein near the wrist. "Take deep breaths," the anesthetist says. "Take deep breaths." He sounds impatient and faintly annoyed. Kevin realizes that, unknowingly, he has been holding his breath. So now he breathes deeply, not to hasten unconsciousness but to keep the anesthetist from being angry with him. The arms of the anesthetist are covered with thick, orange hair. The hair on Kevin's arms is so thin and light as to be almost invisible. Then, suddenly, it seems the lights have been turned down, and sounds come from farther away. The rush of oblivion is like an unexpected and overwhelming nausea. . .

At first he is simply aware of being conscious, only that and nothing more. His mind is restored, but his senses seem dormant. Then it seems to him that one of his ears is missing. He wants very much to be angry about this. His mind says, *the bastards, they must have known in advance that they were going to slice it off; they must have told Terry, and she must have agreed to keep it from me, the bitch.* But he is unable to feel anger; in its place there is an all-encompassing, infantile self-pity.

There are thunderous sea-sounds in his eardrum from which he can never hope to escape. For as long as he lives, there will be this roaring in his eardrum and one day, if he does not kill himself, it will drive him crazy. This is what he imagines.

Then he touches his teeth with his tongue. Bits of enamel fall away. *Merciful Jesus! What else have they done to me?* The slightest pressure of his tongue knocks slivers off his teeth, slivers that crumble into dust and mingle with his saliva. A paste formed from powdered bone and spittle runs down his throat and threatens to choke him.

He lies in bed in the longest room he has ever seen. At the end of this room he sees, as though through the wrong end of a pair of binoculars, two nurses seated at opposite ends of a table. They appear to be sorting papers. From time to time, a telephone rings and one of them answers it. He hears their voices very clearly, but nothing that they say makes sense to him. Nearby a child is crying.

He realizes that he is unutterably thirsty. "Water," he says. "Water."

"No," someone answers.

"Water," he says again. "Water." Never before has he needed anything so desperately. He realizes that prior to this moment he has never truly experienced desire. The craving for water so permeates his being that he ceases to be a man and becomes instead a personification of thirst. If he were handed a glass of water in the certain knowledge that it would kill him, he would drain it without a second thought. "Water," he says. "I'll do anything. Please. Water. I'll never ask for anything again."

Over a period of several hours he again and again reaches what he believes to be the ultimate thirst and goes beyond it to a thirst that is even greater.

Every fifteen minutes they check his blood pressure; each time he begs for water, sometimes with the devious logic of a cunning lunatic, sometimes with the abandon of an hysterical child, sometimes with the monotonous persistence of a despairing animal.

Much later, he becomes aware of the intravenous tubes and the catheters: the drop, pause, drop, pause, of the intravenous fluid entering his arm; the drop, drop, drop of the urine leaving his bladder through a catheter. There are catheters in his shoulders too, sucking out a liquid that is the colour of port wine, flecked with specks of black, dried blood. It is this sucking that creates the sea-sounds, which are nothing like as loud as he at first supposed.

"It's funny," he says, "I thought they had cut off my ear. And my teeth; I thought they had done something to my teeth."

"Mr. O'Brien, dear," the nurse calls him. "Mr.

O'Brien, dear, it's very important that you keep moving your feet." She praises him extravagantly when he finally succeeds in doing so. "That's wonderful," she tells him. "That's really great." She will praise him more fulsomely when he manages to urinate without the assistance of the catheter, will even summon an orderly to admire the contents of the urinal. "Monroe, come here and see this. Isn't that marvellous?" And Kevin will laugh: how many other men possess such skill in urinating that they are applauded for it? Perhaps he could make it his life's work. He would urinate with such ease and in such copious quantities that his picture would be printed on the cover of the *Canadian Medical Journal.*

The Demerol does not kill the pain, but it frees the mind, so that when he is lucky he can look at it almost with detachment. "It's getting worse now," he thinks. "Much worse. In a little while it will be very bad indeed." And yet, as he thinks this, he remains as placid as the face of the the Grand Master of the Dragon Tong in an old movie starring Christopher Lee. *Englishman, perhaps you have heard of the scraping of bones? No? I ask you to do me the honour of inspecting these steel needles. The wound they leave in the flesh is almost imperceptible, even when the bone is scraped to the marrow. Han, I beg you to demonstrate these instruments for the edification of our guest.*

He is almost afraid that such flippancy will offend whatever power it is that controls the waxing and waning of the pain. What if the power should decide to show him that hitherto it has merely been teasing him? When put into words such a fear is ridiculous, but of course he put it into words only when he had stopped being afraid.

There was another game he played with the pain. It was a childish game and, at another level of consciousness, he supposed it showed what a posturing fool he was at heart. In this game, he resolved to bear the pain in the spirit of an Irish Prince of the House of Brian of the

Tributes, like a descendant of Murchadh, whose great axe was the terror of the spear Danes, and of Turloch, his son, whose last act as he fell dying in the water was to grasp an enemy, so that when his corpse was recovered his hands still clutched a drowned Viking's hair.

Kevin O'Brien's grandfather, equally foolish, had died as a charity case in a tuberculosis sanitorium, leaving a pocket watch, five greenish pennies, and a Last Will and Testament that began, "I Cathal, Prince of Fortara," using the title which had been his ancestors', he said, until the Normans conquered Carlow.

The corridor is one hundred feet long, and at the farthest end of it, under a window and between two large potted plants, there is an empty armchair with maroon upholstery. Possibly it is one of several chairs; if so, Kevin ignores the others so completely that, for his purpose, they do not exist.

He is walking for the first time since the operation, and if he succeeds in reaching the maroon chair he will be free to sit down in it; even healthy persons sit down in chairs. On the other hand, he cannot stop when part way there and sit on the floor, no matter how badly he may need to do so. Above all, he must not faint. This test is self-imposed; but resembles many medical tests in that it devolves upon a matter of etiquette, the substitution of an artificial restraint for an involuntary one.

Each step is a separate and distinct event.

Each yard he covers is an ambition achieved.

A step begins when you throw all your weight on one leg and balance on it. You lift the other foot slowly, an act that starts in the hip and moves down through thigh, calf and ankle.

It is imperative that the knee of the leg on which you are balancing remains stiff until almost the very instant when the other foot returns to the floor.

After each step, you stand with your feet together and

take a deep breath. And you stay very close to the wall; because when you start to lose your balance a wall can be the most important thing in the world.

As a child, he had stood on his head and pretended that he was walking on the ceiling, and in a little while it had seemed that he was walking upright in an inverted room in which the floor was bare except for a lamp, while chairs and a table were glued or nailed to the ceiling.

Then, through an open doorway, he glimpses two old men. They are in bed and one of them appears to have screws fixed in his skull above his ears, so that it is as if his head were in a vice; he observes the world only through mirrors, and it is in a mirror that he sees Kevin passing.

"God, that's a big bastard," the mirror man says. "I'd sure as hell hate to tangle with him."

"I don't know about that," his companion replies. "Most of those big guys are pretty slow on their feet."

"Maybe they're slow," the mirror man concedes. "But you've sure as hell had it if one of them gets a hold on you."

It is as if these were the first human voices he has heard in months. He laughs aloud at the thought of an old man with his head in a vice sizing him up as a possible opponent in a wrestling match.

*I'm erect, he thinks. I'm erect and walking. I'm alive!* He can scarcely lift his feet, and yet inwardly he is dancing.

He reaches the armchair, and with the theatrical vanity of a child, pauses defiantly before sitting down. The sunlight from the window is very bright. As soon as he can breathe without gasping, he turns to look out at the grass.

# MORNING
# FLIGHT
# TO RED DEER

*ON THE BUS* to the Calgary airport, he sat across the aisle from a woman who had no matches. He liked her because she smiled with him at the country-and-western song on the driver's portable radio. "Please, God, don't let my divorce be granted," wailed, hollered, communicated by Miss Kitty Wells of the Grand Ole Opry with such absolute conviction that, for the moment, he loved everybody who did not know that it was ridiculous. There were permanent frown lines in the forehead of the woman who had no matches, which meant that she probably came from the working class, as he had. The middle classes are not necessarily happier, but smiling is habitual with them, a polite gesture. So, by the age of thirty, when the lines are there even when the expression is not, it is usually easy to distinguish the members of one class from the other, or so he believed.

"Could I have a light, please?" she said, holding up her cigarette as people do when they ask for a light, as if to bear witness that they are not pyromaniacs. Her cigarette lit, they exchanged the meaningless phrases that sometimes, not often, open the way for a genuine conversation. "It looks like a good day for flying," he said. And she said that 7 a.m. was one hell of an hour at which to schedule a flight.

He learned, somewhat to his disappointment, that she had not been smiling with him, after all, but at something which he had not noticed and which would not have amused him. "That nutty driver scared that old dude with the dog almost to death." When they boarded the plane for Red Deer, he found that they had been assigned neighbouring seats. "Do you live in Red Deer?" he asked, unable to think of anything else.

"God, no, I'm from Calgary." It was obvious that she thought his question stupid. Well, most Calgarians were extraordinarily self-conscious about being city-dwellers, doubtless because so many of them had escaped there from a countryside where billboards warned motorists that The Steps of the Fornicator Lead Down to Hell. During his visit there, he had come to suspect that nothing would make them prouder than more traffic jams, more muggings, more pollution — anything that reminded them that, by God, they had got out of Buffalo Wallow.

They were in flight. Her hair smelled of lime-scented shampoo. "Could I borrow your lighter again, please?" She was a deliberate chain smoker, he had observed, not the nervous kind. This time when he reached into his jacket pocket he found a book of Travel Lodge matches. "M'lady," he said, with a little bow, "may I present you with your very own matches?"

"Thanks." He was startled by the anger in her voice and the finality with which she turned away from him. Should he apologize for having thought that she might come from a hick town? When he brushed against her, while reaching for a magazine — air travel causes strangers to touch in a way that our ancestors would have deemed unseemly in a couple engaged to be married — he felt little electric shocks of hostility. Suddenly, he realized that it was not Red Deer; it was the matches.

"Look," he would have liked to say to her. "I wasn't being sarcastic. I don't begrudge you the use of my lighter, for God's sake. I was merely trying to be mildly amusing." But he was not the kind of person who could offer such explanations and have them accepted.

"Excuse me," she said. He stood up as best he could to let her pass. Her buttocks pressed hard against his groin. There was a mole on the back of her neck. Her ear-lobes had been pierced. She did not come back.

"Would you care for tea or coffee, sir?" The stewardess was smiling, of course, but in her eyes, as in the eyes of many stewardesses, there was the glint of cruelty which comes from belonging to a sorority that works in an environment which throws the sense of reality slightly askew. It was funny how the airlines had dressed their stewardesses in shorter and shorter dresses and then, just before their panties would have become visible, had decided that the dresses were in fact jackets, to be worn with slacks. He had three ways of entertaining himself on planes, aside from reading or drinking. One of them was creating erotic fantasies.

Was it possible that the woman without matches felt that he had rejected her as a woman? Shutting his eyes, he willed time to run backwards, willed the woman back into the seat beside him, willed her to resemble Lauren Bacall.

It didn't work. It was too early in the day. And he wasn't in the right mood to make up limericks, which was another way he had of passing the time on planes and in dentists' waiting rooms. He raised the arm-rest on the vacant seat beside him, drank his coffee and began to play his third form of mental solitaire, eavesdropping.

It was much preferable to conversing with strangers. He could turn the dial in his head toward the seats to his right, the seats ahead or the seats behind him. He could tune in and tune out whenever he liked. It was like using a scanner radio, he supposed, except that no desk sergeant or cab dispatcher was ever likely to sound as passionate as the man in front of him now, who was saying:

"Wait a minute . . . What it appeared to be . . . Can I finish? When Dad passed away — I more than willingly —. He did a good job of administering things — very little direct control. The only kind of feedback —. The prime agitator, for want of a better word, was Phyllis. At times I questioned Phyll's loyalty —. I was still suffering from some kind of kid brother complex. For example —."

Had there been a quarrel over a will? As often happened, two people were talking, but only one voice was distinguishable. The man who had once suffered from a kid brother complex was playing a trumpet solo; his companion was merely his accompanist.

The trumpet kept shifting back and forth between whine and bluster. Anyone who said, "Can I finish?" was a boor as well as a bore. Perhaps something less depressing was happening elsewhere. He gave his empty coffee cup and plastic spoon to the stewardess and tuned in the seats behind him.

This time it was a duet. "How long has he been with us?" one voice said. It was a very confident, masculine voice. A boardroom voice. This was the kind of passenger who carried an attaché case and, normally, spent the flight leafing through sheets of xeroxed paper.

"I have his file with me," another voice said. This one was much like the other, but younger and a shade less confident. Yes, there was the click of an attaché case being opened, the rustle of papers being gone through. "Here it is. Yes I thought so. He came to us straight out of law school. Fifteen year ago."

"Fifteen years — and never in a bigger town than Red Deer?"

"Right."

"I would have thought he'd have got the message long ago."

"I'm sure he would have if he had ever asked for something better and been turned down. The man's no fool. The thing is, he's never applied for a promotion —at least not in my time."

"No ambition."

"He's a funny guy. I wouldn't call him lazy exactly. But he never *does* anything. Doesn't golf, doesn't play tennis, doesn't even jog as far as I know. Won't get involved in the community —"

"I know the type. Married?"

"Very much so. That's a big part of the problem."

"Ah. What is it? Her tongue, her bladder, her belly or her crotch?"

"I beg your pardon?"

"Does she talk too much, drink too much, eat too much, or screw too much?"

"Oh!" followed by laughter that said the younger man would be careful, when they came to a door, to see that the older man passed through first. "Nothing like that. It's just that she — well, let me put it this way, she doesn't chew gum but she always looks as if she's about to pop a stick in her mouth."

"I think I get the picture."

"Don't get me wrong. It's not just the wife. And it's not just his lack of drive — "

"Balls."

"Pardon?"

"You call it drive, I call it balls."

"Right. Well, it's not just his lack of balls. There's a helluva lot more to it than that. There's what happened at the office party, for instance —"

"SIT DOWN, MICHAEL!" This was the woman across the aisle, knocking all other stations off the air. The child she had rebuked burst into tears. "I'm sorry, darling." The woman reached out to comfort the child; the child pulled away, his sobs of hurt changing to sobs of anger. "I said, I was sorry, darling." This child sobbed louder. "Here. See what Mummy's got for you." She had taken candy from her purse. The child continued to cry, but now his sobs were purely physical; his mind was on another matter: how to satisfy greed without relinquishing anger. After a moment of indecision, he snatched the candy and stuffed it into his mouth.

"I had to do a lot of explaining after that one," the younger executive was saying.

"I'll just bet you did. My God!" Then a pause, after which the older executive said, "My God!" again.

They both laughed. The older man's amusement sounded genuine. "Of course you could get your own ass burnt on this one," he said.

"I don't see —"

"If you really don't see, then you deserve to get your ass burnt. Good God, man, you've been working with the guy for — how long?"

"Three years," the younger man admitted, miserably.

"Three years," the older man repeated mercilessly. "That means that when our boy gets the chop, the boys in Winnipeg will be asking a helluva lot of questions — and some of them will be about you."

"I suppose you're right."

"You know damn well I'm right. It's not going to look too damn good for me, either. Jesus, I'm supposed to be on top of these things." A pause. "It would solve a lot of problems if he'd do it himself. Do you think there's any chance of that?"

"If you had asked me that a year ago, I wouldn't have had to think about it for an instant. He'd have taken the hint then. Now, I don't know."

"It's that bad?"

"It's that bad."

"Does he know I'm coming?"

"No."

"Well, he'll know that something's up as soon as he sees me." Another pause. "Maybe I ought to surprise him."

"That just might work." The younger man sounded almost desperately relieved.

"It's worth a try," the older man said.

"The best time would be at lunch," said the younger man. "After he's got a couple of martinis into him."

"Enough rope," said the older man.

"Enough rope," the younger man repeated. It was as if they were toasting each other.

"Ladies and gentlemen, we are beginning our descent," said the loudspeaker.

"Poor bastard," thought the eavesdropper, whom we will henceforth call Smith, which is as good a name as any.

As they disembarked — "deplaned," the stewardess would have said — Smith tried not to look at the two executives. He knew perfectly well that he was being absurd; but he couldn't help thinking that if their eyes met his and they saw the dislike in his face, they would know immediately that he had been spying on them.

It was impossible to shut them out completely, of course; as they brushed past him on the tarmac — such men were always in a hurry — he saw that one wore eye-glasses, the other a moustache.

"Phyll, darling! You didn't have to meet me at this outrageous hour, I could have taken a cab." This from the man who had once suffered from a kid brother complex to a woman with badly dyed hair.

"My God," said the younger executive, the one with the moustache.

"What is it?" said the one in eye-glasses. Like Smith, they were waiting at the baggage carousel.

"It's the wife. Heading toward the exit. The woman

with the cigarette. I thought that face was familiar, but I couldn't place it until now."

It was the woman whom Smith had offended with his offer of matches, the woman who had refused to admit that she lived in Red Deer.

"You don't think —"

"Not a chance. Just after we took off, she went to the back of the plane."

"Funny you didn't recognize her then."

"I've only seen her a couple of times before. And she looks like every waitress in every greasy spoon in the country."

"Yes. I see what you mean."

Smith snatched up his suitcase and hurried after her

She had boarded the bus. Good. The executives were certain to hire a cab. Smith, too, boarded the bus. Fate had provided an empty seat beside her. He sat down in it.

"Hello," he said.

"Hi."

"Look, I wasn't being sarcastic. About the matches, I mean."

"What?"

"Back there on the plane, I wasn't being sarcastic when I offered you the matches. You thought I was, but I wasn't."

"I don't know what in hell you're talking about."

"It's not important. The important thing is —" He knew by now that he was making an absolute fool of himself; the woman eyed him with that shrivelling female contempt which created the legends of Circe and Medusa; but it was too late for him to stop, "— the important thing is that your husband's boss is out to get him. I overhead them talking about it on the plane —"

"Get lost, you creep."

"But —"

"Driver!"

"This guy bothering you, lady?"

"He's some kind of nut. Just make him go away."

"You heard the lady, Mac. Beat it."

Smith stood up unsteadily, half-blinded by the stares of the other passengers. When he took his suitcase from the overhead rack, it seemed twice as heavy as before. He got off the bus, colliding with a passenger who was getting on — "Hey! Watch what you're doing, Buddy" — and looked around him for a cab that would take him to the merciful sanctuary of an hotel.

"That's what would have happened," he told himself as he unpacked his shirts and underwear. "That, or something very much like it." But perhaps he could have telephoned to the intended victim. "You don't know me. But listen carefully. They're out to get you."

"Who is this?"

"That doesn't matter. Let's just say I'm a friend. I flew up from Calgary on the same plane as —"

"Who is this?"

"Please stop asking, 'Who is this?' and listen to me. I flew up from Calgary on the same plane as —"

CLICK!

That was even sillier than thinking he ought to tell the woman on the bus. How could he telephone the poor sod when he didn't know his name, or even the name of the company he worked for?

There was nothing at all he could have done. Anyway, the fellow probably deserved to be fired; and if he didn't deserve it, it could turn out to be the best thing that had ever happened to him.

Smith telephoned room service and ordered coffee and a sandwich. He tried to force the conversation which he had overheard on the plane out of his mind, tried even harder to stop himself from thinking, "What if somewhere out there, they're making plans to get me?"

# ABOUT MEMORIALS

*THIS AFTERNOON I* gave a reading of my poems at the Balmoral Public Library. Max Worthington drove over to the Halifax Airport to pick me up. As the plane landed, I thought of my father as I always do when landing or taking off at Halifax or Saint John. My father worked at both airports when they were being built in the late 1940s. He was a plumber's assistant, which means that, using a pick and shovel, he dug trenches for pipes and after the pipes were laid filled the trenches in. My sister and I lived at home in Lockhartville, just the two of us. In 1947, when he worked at Halifax, she was twelve and I was fourteen. Each week we mailed him the sales slips from the general store where we bought groceries — dinner was potatoes and a tin of peas or a tin of corn or, less often, a tin of a lunchmeat called *Klek* — having altered the totals at the bottom of the slips with a pencil and an eraser so that he wouldn't know how much he owed. We weren't embezzlers, Stephanie and I; we simply wished to postpone the inescapable ritual in which our father first stamped about the kitchen, cursing and lunging out with his fists and feet at the chairs, the table, the couch, the stove, the wood-box and the doors, as if they were all of them capable both of feeling pain and of purposely inflicting it; and then slumped down in a chair, usually by the window that faced the dirt road, less often by the window that faced the well, and sat there in stony silence, with his back toward us, shutting us out, because as he said, it cost so God damn, God damn much to feed us.

"I've become a senior citizen since the last time you saw me," Max said. He was smaller than I'd remembered him. Mrs. Forrester would be at the reading, he told me. "She says you're the only person she ever knew who read *War and Peace* in a week." One of my old schoolteachers would be there as well. Phyllis Rhodenizer — did I remember her?

"She gave me an 'F' for a composition in Grade Four. Said I'd obviously copied it out of a book."

"You've got an amazing memory," Max said. "If I'd had your memory I might have done something with my life." I couldn't think of anything to say to that. I'd always thought of Max as being rather pleased with himself. "Do you ever get back to Lockhartville?" he asked.

"I haven't been there since my father died."

"That would be — what, two, three years ago?"

"Seven."

"Seven years." He shook his head ruefully. "It's frightening how time flies when you're my age." There was a four-lane highway between Halifax and Balmoral now.

Short stretches of woods, mostly evergreen, separated the farms, each with its white and green or white and black house, gray outbuildings and green pasture containing black and white cattle. "Got any new books coming out?"

"Not right away."

"I saw your last play on TV. That's where the money is, eh? In TV."

"Only in the States."

"That right? You must be doing okay, though. Moneywise, I mean." He chuckled. "That's not the polite thing to say, is it? But you know me."

The truth is, Max Worthington and I don't know each other. We never have. Yet if anyone were to ask, I'd say, "Oh, sure, I know Max Worthington; I've know him for more than thirty years," and it would not be a lie but rather one of those simplifications without which casual conversation would be next to impossible.

When we engage in such simplifications long enough or often enough we come to mistake them for facts. I'd never have accepted an invitation to give a reading at Balmoral if it hadn't been Max who telephoned me. I don't like to go back to places I've left, probably because it has always been so hard for me to screw up the courage to leave. But that night I'd had several stiff drinks of gin and here was Max on the telephone saying, "They've elected me president of the Eclectic Reading Club we have here. It was founded by Sir Charles G. D. Roberts, incidentally, when he was a schoolmaster at the Anglican boys' school. Oscar Wilde spoke at one of its early meetings, during his tour of North America." Here Max inserted the obligatory joke about Wilde. Then, "It would mean a lot to me if you'd accept. Of course I'm afraid we couldn't afford to pay you your usual fee, just expenses." I suppose he had read in *People* that Allen Ginsberg got $5,000 an appearance, and hadn't I been photographed with Allen Ginsberg and the picture published in *Maclean's*?

"That's okay," I said.

"Does that mean you'll come?"

"Yes."

"Great!"

*It's bigger than I remember it*, I thought, as Max brought his Volvo to a stop in front of a long two-storey sandstone building. "I haven't been inside that building for more than twenty-five years," I said.

"There's been a lot of water gone under the bridge since then."

"Yes."

We country boys and girls came into town only on Saturday nights, a bunch of us on the back of somebody's pick-up truck. Once, and I smiled at the memory, when there was no half-ton available, my Aunt Agnes hitched a tractor to a farm waggon and transported a bunch of us to town in it. Balmoral to me then wasn't just a little market town, where farmers loaded their apples on to railway cars and bought machines with which to spray insecticides on their orchards; it was a feast of lights.

Neon lights outside, fluorescent lights inside. Overhead signs, show windows, traffic signals, pinball machines, jukeboxes, all of them brimming over with light. At home in Lockhartville, eighteen miles away, fifteen of them by dirt road, we used kerosene lamps and if you had to go to the backhouse after dark you lit a kerosene lantern and took it with you.

I had forgotten: the long two-storey building wasn't the public library. It was the War Memorial Community Centre. The library was merely a room in the Centre, off a hallway in which teenagers brushed past us on their way, Max explained, to the swimming pool or the badminton court or the games room. I've seen bigger libraries in high schools.

"The books all look so new," I said. Back when I used to come here every Saturday night, between visiting Cameron's Book Store, which also sold greeting cards and wallpaper and where, aside from hardcover Bibles and Missals, the only books were paperback Penguins and Pocketbooks (which sold for twenty-five cents, the same amount as the minimum legal hourly wage that I got paid for working in the sawmill at Lockhartville), and going to the show at the Imperial Theatre which almost always featured a Western, practically all of the books in the library were old, and had been privately donated. There were 19th century editions of Darwin, Marx and Herbert Spencer, in which the pages were still uncut until I got them home.

Now there was a shelf of the current best-sellers, a stack filled with books labelled with a skull to indicate that they were detective stories, another stack filled with books labelled with a maple leaf to show that they were Canadian. Cookbooks, books on the care and training of dogs, books on how to make quilts and tie knots . . .

"We're part of the Douglas County Regional Libraries System now," Max said expansively. "Nothing like it was in your day, eh?"

"No."

I had met Max for the first time in this room. Mrs. Forrester, the librarian (the only one) introduced us. "This young man wants to be a writer."

Max wore a grayish tweed sports jacket. I'm sure of this because I kept my eyes on his jacket all the time we talked, being too shy even at sixteen to look a stranger in the face. He wore a grayish tweed sports jacket today as well. This one had frayed cuffs and the nap was badly worn. I'd not have noticed that when I was sixteen.

"Lockhartville, eh?" He had asked where I lived and I had told him. "Let's see what you've got there." I let him take my armload of books. A bizarre collection, no doubt. While most of the donors had favoured the nineteenth-century English classics, several must have had eccentric tastes. "Pretty heavy stuff. So you want to be a writer. What kind of writer do you want to be?"

"I don't know," I said miserably. It was like the time when I was four or five years old and tied a rope to a white birch and all of a sudden the white birch turned into a wild white stallion, as I had known it would. "I don't know," I answered, red-faced, when my Wicked Uncle appeared from Nowhere, as Wicked Uncles do, and asked me what I thought I was doing.

I knew perfectly well what kind of a writer I wanted to be. I wanted to be a poet like Keats and to die in Rome. coughing up blood, an eternity from now when I was middle-aged and twenty-six.

"Tell you what," Max said on that Saturday night so long ago. "Next time you're in town, drop into the *Plain Dealer* office and we'll have a chin-wag." The *Plain Dealer* was the weekly newspaper (circulation 2,000) of which he was editor and publisher.

"Great!" I said, and because I tended to repeat things then, "Great!"

"We'll see you in Fleet Street yet," Mrs. Forrester said afterwards. She was English. I thought of her as being akin to Beatrice Webb: an intellectual and the mentor of intellectuals. She published articles in the *Family Herald.* Her husband, whom I never met, was always applying for some important-sounding job, such as postmaster or county sheriff. I was never quite clear as to what he did in the meantime.

"We're a trifle early," Max said now. "How about a bite of lunch?"

"That sounds fine." I needed a drink. A double martini, straight up, with two olives, and I'd be better prepared to face the past. But Max led me to the Community Centre cafeteria which wasn't even licensed to sell beer. I drank black coffee while he ate his half-order of Chili Con Carne. "They're good here that way," he said. "They'll serve you a half-order if you ask for it and only charge you half-price." I had convinced him that, on second thought, I wasn't hungry. "Don't tell me you've got butterflies in your tummy," he chuckled. "A celebrity like you must be used to being lionized by now."

"I'm not a celebrity," I said. "I'm just world famous in Lockhartville and Balmoral."

"Mrs. Forrester says you're the only genius she ever produced."

I laughed. Max eyed me with disapproval. "She means it," he said. He glanced at his watch. "I think it's time we were on our way."

The first time I called on Max at the *Plain Dealer*, he told me about a recent meeting with Lord Beaverbrook, who in those days visited the Maritimes several times a year. "I made up my mind about one thing before I ever knocked on the door of his hotel suite; I wasn't going to give him a chance to dismiss me —"

"To dismiss you?"

"To end the conversation whenever he felt like it and send me away as if he were the King and I was a foot-man," Max explained impatiently. "He's famous for doing that. He never says goodbye when he's talking to you on the telephone, you know. He just hangs up on you. Every time. Well, as I say, I'd made up my mind that I wasn't going to give him a chance to dismiss *me* —"

I'm sure Max must have succeeded. Otherwise, he'd not have told me the story. But I don't recall how he managed it. Probably I wasn't listening. Not because I was bored, but because I was so excited. To think that I was talking with a newspaper publisher who had talked with Lord Beaverbrook, who was a friend of Winston Churchill's, who . . . This wasn't snobbery, it was awe. Except for those Saturday night trips to Balmoral, I had scarcely been outside of Lockhartville.

Always after that, I tried, not always successfully, to avoid giving Max an opportunity to dismiss *me*.

The reading wasn't in the library — there wasn't space for it there — but in another room off the same hallway. It was the usual set-up, with a lectern facing a hundred or so uncomfortable-looking folding chairs, and a table at the back on which there was a large coffee urn, stacks of styrofoam cups, paper napkins, a jar of powdered cream, little packets of sugar, and little wooden thingamajigs with which to stir the coffee.

I wished I hadn't come.

The audience was older than at most poetry readings. Some of the women wore hats; most of the men were in suits. They smiled a little shyly and sat very stiffly in their uncomfortable chairs, like children when they're awaiting a new experience and, at the last moment, have begun to wonder if they've been told the whole truth about what to expect.

Max bustled about in the manner characteristic of amateur impresarios. I sat down in the front row. Anywhere else in Canada, I'd have regarded this as simply another gathering of fairly typical members of the small town middle-classes. The people in this audience would differ from their neighbours only in that they joined the Book-of-the-Month Club and claimed to watch nothing on TV except the Public Broadcasting Service. Here in Balmoral, I was reluctantly aware that they belonged to another tribe than the one in which I grew up. Their tribe was known collectively to my father and others like him as *The Big Man*. "He got out of this big car, wearin' this big white shirt and smokin' this jeezly big cigar ..." *The Big Man* could be the local buyer of pulpwood for the paper mill — the man with the big cigar — or the manager of the paper mill or the owner himself, who lived in Halifax and might as well have lived on Olympus. What mattered was his being *The Big Man*, just as what mattered about a Jew was his being a Jew.

We were every bit as different from the middle-classes as if they had been white and we had been Indians.

Max stood beside me and had begun to speak. "— an internationally known author who got his start right here in Balmoral —"

"Lockhartville," someone interjected.

"Well, Lockhartville is a suburb of Balmoral, after all," Max said. He paused expectantly. There was a little ripple of laughter. "Ladies and gentlemen, I have to admit in all modesty that I'm a little proud that I'm the guy who recommended this fellow for his first job on a weekly newspaper. Some people would have said that I was taking a pretty big chance, considering that he'd never worked on a newspaper before, hadn't even gone to high school, for that matter; but I knew better. I could see that he had the stuff in him that it takes to succeed."

Oh, Max, Max. Don't you remember how it really was? That little son of a bitch from Lockhartville stole some of your envelopes and letterhead, then wrote his own references, to which he signed your name. Perhaps you never knew that. If you had known, I think perhaps you'd have felt it was your duty to warn any prospective employer and possibly to notify the police. I recall your telling me how you went to the RCMP after a known Communist — you called him a known Communist — asked you to print something for him in your job printing plant. "Don't turn him down," the RCMP said. "Quote him a price he can't possibly afford. Soak him. That's what everybody else does." You told me this story in the course of warning me against associating with that same known Communist who also happened to be a fine poet. "There's no money in poetry," was another thing you used to say. And, with dour satisfaction, "You won't find any time to fiddle around with poems when you're working full-time on a weekly newspaper." This last bit of advice was given to me just before I left for another province to take a job I had acquired on the strength of the references to which I had forged your name.

At last, Max finished his introduction, not of me but of the person he imagined me to be: a great writer who, at least in part, was his creation. "Thank you, Max," I said and began to read verses.

I had read six or seven when my father, dead for seven years, walked in and sat down in the back row.

*Uncle David.*

He had always stood very straight, with his shoulders thrown back and his chin tilted upwards. His eyes had taken momentary possession of everything they touched; a glance from him, coupled with his lordly grin, was enough to entrap a woman or benumb a small boy. Now he slouched, as my father had, and seemed to have shrunk so that, incredibly, he was now no taller than my father had been.

Aunt Agnes had sat down beside him. A large woman, not fat, but with enormous bones, she sat with her knees wide apart, leaning forward, her elbows resting on the back of the empty chair in front of her.

Somehow, I managed to keep on reading. I've read so many times that it's almost like driving a car; I can switch from one emotion to another as absently as I shift gears. Sometimes this worries me and I fight against it. This afternoon I was grateful. My mouth and throat were dry, and my hands shook so that I didn't dare to pick up the glass of water in front of me.

I got through it. There was applause. Max stood up again. *Dear God.* What was he blathering on about now?

"When I introduced him earlier, I said that he got his start in Balmoral. Actually, he got his start right here in this very building. In our Public Library. I think it would be most appropriate if our former librarian, Mrs. Gwendolyn Forrester, said a few words at this time."

Mrs. Forrester came to the front. She wore a black wool suit with leg-of-mutton sleeves and a little pill-box hat. Just as in the old days, the ear-pieces of her eyeglasses were connected across the back of her neck by a black cord. Her accent was different from how I remembered it. Not Oxford-Cambridge, as I had thought, but north of England, probably Yorkshire. She said now that I was the only person she had known who had read *War and Peace* in a week. She said I was the only genius she had ever produced. "There was a special aura about him when he was a mere stripling," she said. There was indeed. There was a special aura about everyone who wintered in a house where the lack of central heating and indoor plumbing made it made it next to impossible to take a bath.

"As much as we might like to, we of the Balmoral Public Library can't take all the credit for this young man's success," Mrs. Forrester said. "So, I think it would be very appropriate if we now heard from an old school-teacher of his, Mrs. Phyllis Rhodenizer."

More applause. Mrs. Rhodenizer wore a pink polyester suit with a cameo brooch at the neck of her flowered blouse. "He was the best pupil I ever had," she said.

I grimaced, calling up that little boy the other kids called Rabbit because, never having been taught to blow his nose properly, he sniffed constantly as a rabbit does, and who feared and hated school so much that in Grade 5, the year Mrs. Rhodenizer taught in Lockhartville, he was there to say, "Present," when the roll was called only thirty-seven times during the entire year.

She went on to tell how we kids in Lockhartville came to the one-room school in our bare feet. That much was true. We went barefoot from May until October. She described the wood-stove and told how in winter we spread our mittens on the sheet of tin under it to dry, and of the well from which we fetched our water: there was a bucket at the back of the room with a single white enamel mug from which we all drank. She didn't mention the two outdoor privies, one for girls and one for boys.

"Our guest of honour is living proof, if any further proof is needed, that those little white schoolhouses turned out some great men."

Max beamed. Mrs. Forrester dabbed at her eyes with a Kleenex. Uncle David and Aunt Agnes looked as if they were in church and their nephew — no, their son — was being consecrated Bishop. I felt as though I had swindled the innocent. Then I felt angry. What right did they have to create this caricature of me to give fictitious support to their self-esteem?

There was worse to come.

"I take great pleasure in announcing that henceforth and for ever the Balmoral Public Library will bear the name of the renowned Canadian poet, author and playwright who is its most distinguished alumnus, as he is my most distinguished alumnus."

Then came a standing ovation. It was like my father's funeral when I came close to breaking into hysterical laughter over the presiding minister's pedantic diction, which reminded me of the hilarious scene in Cecil B. DeMille's *The Ten Commandments,* where a disembodied voice enunciates the words while bolts of lightning engrave them on tablets of stone. Once, years before, I had burst into laughter when my father and I were lost in the woods. "Boy, I swear to God, you ain't got a brain in your head," he had said to me then. I could imagine him muttering the same thing as he lay in his coffin — a thought that made it even harder to keep a straight face as the minister droned on about the "Cree-ate-TOR."

At the funeral, if the laughter had come, I planned to cover my face with my hands in hope that the others would think I wept aloud. This would have disgusted them too, especially the men and most especially Uncle David — "My God, a nephew of mine bawling like some damn wog" — but it might not have disgusted them so much.

After the plaque was unveiled, everyone shook my hand. I felt a little drunk, although I'd had nothing to drink. It's the way I usually feel when something unforeseen and unsettling happens, such as having my car hit a patch of ice and skid off the road. I doubt if anyone in the audience had read anything I've written except magazine articles. Several mentioned the *Reader's Digest* or said they'd seen one of my plays on TV. Max introduced me to the local member of the provincial Legislature. He also introduced him to Uncle David and Aunt Agnes. "This is a real pleasure," Uncle David said, pumping the politician's hand, and it was plain from his tone and expression that he meant it. A few moments later, when we became separated, I saw that my uncle was sticking close to the politician, and at one point overheard him say, "I knew there was something special about the young fellow right from the start. Always had his nose in a book. Always scribbling. It was me that brought him and Max together. Max and me are brother Knights of Pythias. So I know Max pretty well. I'll never forget the day I took the young fellow into Max's office and introduced them —."

"He's dying," Aunt Agnes said to me.

"What?"

"Your Uncle David. He's dying. Of cancer. Like your father."

"But he seems so full of life." It was true. Talking with the politician and other members of the tribe of *The Big Man*, he looked from a little distance away like his old self, shoulders thrown back, chin tilted upwards, grinning.

"He's been flat on his back in bed for weeks. But today I had to help him get dressed and drive him into town. He wouldn't take 'no' for an answer."

"I could have got Max to drive me out to Lockhartville to see him if I'd known."

"That wouldn't have been the same. He wanted to be here. For the ceremony."

"I don't want to interrupt," Mrs. Rhodenizer said. "But could I have my picture taken with you?"

"Sure."

"He says it's all right," she told a friend with a Polaroid. I put my arm around her. "Oh!" she said, and put her arm around me. Looking at the picture a few minutes later, I blurted, "We look to be the same age."

"Flatterer," she said. But it was true. Dear God, she

must have been so young when she taught at Lockhart-ville. Perhaps as young as eighteen, surely no older than twenty.

"You must be awfully proud of him," she said to Aunt Agnes. "I know I am."

"Me too," said Uncle David, rejoining us. I saw now that his lips were white from pain and his skin gray from exhaustion.

Max and Mrs. Forrester stood close by. They smiled at me, lovingly.

Would Max and Mrs. Forrester and Mrs. Rhodenizer have even remembered me if I hadn't achieved what they imagined to be Success? I asked myself. It was a rhetorical question. I knew they'd have forgotten me years ago. And, as Aunt Agnes said, Uncle David hadn't got off his deathbed to see me again; he had got off his deathbed so he could talk with a member of the Legislature and other elders of the tribe of *The Big Man*, as an equal, in his own eyes at least.

Only Aunt Agnes was there simply because I was family. No, on second thought, she was there because Uncle David could not have come without her.

I almost wept.

Life had given these people so little that it was important to them to believe they were each of them a part — not of me, but of a person to whom a plaque could be erected. Because I had made this possible, they loved me.

"You're not saying much," Max said.

"Still waters run deep," Mrs. Forrester said.

"You're beautiful," I said to her.

"Humph," she said.

"It's time you and me hit the road, old boy," Aunt Agnes said to Uncle David. He put his hands to his head and groaned. "David, are you all right?"

"Of course I'm all right; that groan was for the way you drive."

She slapped at him playfully. "You," she said.

"She doesn't have any driver's licence," he said. "Tried three times and couldn't pass the test."

"You'll have people believing your nonsense," she said, helping him with his coat.

"I could drive you out to Lockhartville," I said. "Max could follow us in his car and drive me back."

"Nonsense," Aunt Agnes said. "I got us here, and I can get us back."

As they pulled out of the parking lot, they knocked over an empty garbage can and sent it rolling. They drove off with Aunt Agnes leaning on the horn and waving.

"They're quite a pair," Max said.

"Yes."

Something astonishing had happened a few minutes earlier. I hugged my uncle for the first time in my life — and this is the astonishing thing — he did not back away and crack the mandatory joke about fairies, he hugged me back.

As my plane took off, it came back to me that when my father worked at the airports in Halifax and Saint John the construction sites had wonderfully romantic postal addresses: Loch Lomond and Waverley. It also came back to me that each of the cheques he mailed to us after receiving those doctored sales slips from the general store was accompanied by a letter written in pencil on a single sheet of lined paper and that the letter always began, "Dear Kids, How are you? I am fine . . ."